WHEEZER
AND THE
ROAD TO GOLD

KITTY SUTTON

Wheezer and the Road to Gold

"In **WHEEZER AND THE PAINTED FROG** Kitty Sutton has penned the first of a delightful series of novels set against the Cherokee removal. Orphaned and exploited in a new land, a young Cherokee girl seeks justice for the murder of her brother and to her aid comes Wheezer, a small white dog with the charm and sensibility to both ferret out the bad guys and bring a sparkling cast of characters together .

We consider Kitty Sutton's novels a tantalizing hook to reel young readers into the magic and enjoyment of our nation's history ."

-W. Michael Gear and Kathleen O'Neal Gear - New York Times bestselling authors of *People of the Morning Star.*

"Once again Kitty Sutton has spun a magical tale in **WHEEZER AND THE SHY COYOTE.** New villains are preying on the Native peoples struggling to build new homes in Oklahoma. Wheezer's beloved 'People' are drawn inexorably into a dangerous web of intrigue as they struggle to stop the insidious whiskey trade. With 'his 'people's' lives on the line, it's up to Wheezer and his curious new friend 'Yellow Eyes', a shy coyote, to break the case open. Steeped in Native American history and lore, **WHEEZER AND THE SHY COYOTE** is a worthy successor in the 'Mystery from the Trail of Tears' series."

-Kathleen O'Neal Gear and W. Michael Gear - *New York Times* bestselling authors of *PEOPLE OF THE SONGTRAIL.*

"WHEEZER AND THE SHY COYOTE is a worthy successor in the 'Mystery from the Trail of Tears' series."

-Kathleen O'Neal Gear and W. Michael Gear - *New York Times* bestselling authors of *PEOPLE OF THE SONGTRAIL.*

"Wheezer and the Painted Frog is at once joyous and heartbreaking. You will ache for the suffering, be outraged by the wrongs, fascinated by the way of life, identify with Sasa and above all you will love Wheezer. You will look for h is spirit in every dog you meet!"

-Anne Perry, Author of *Acceptable Loss*

Kitty Sutton

WHEEZER AND THE ROAD TO GOLD

Written by
Kitty Sutton

Published by
Little Buffalo Arts Publishing

© 2018

Wheezer and the Road to Gold

Front Cover Art: Amanda McCollum
Back Cover Art: Kitty Sutton

This is a work of fiction. Although it is based on real historical events, some characters have been created for the sake of this story. Actual persons have been included, based on documentation of their presence at relevant events, but actual dialogue is speculation, used to enhance the dramatic tension of the story. Certain words and dialects are used which are representative of the point in history in which this story took place, and should be viewed as such.

In an effort to present the broadest view of the events happening in this period, the author has condensed the time line so that some events may not appear in their proper sequence, year or season. Any mistakes made, or omissions of other pertinent events happening during this era are purely the artistic license by the author and may be taken up later in this ongoing saga.

Acknowledgments

I would like to acknowledge the helpful work of my editor, Marilyn M Alvey. She worked long hours to whip my book into shape. She is also a good friend.

Wheezer and the Road to Gold

Dedication

I would like to dedicate this book to my dear brothers and sisters in Jehovah's congregation who have encouraged me and supported me in my endeavor. Writers write in a vacuum of sorts, and their help and opinions are of utmost value to me.

Wheezer and the Road to Gold

xi

Wheezer and the Road to Gold
By Kitty Sutton

Prologue

Mountain sat by the stream with a small bowl he was using to pan for gold. It was all he had after his tools were stolen away the night before. The boy, now only thirteen, was a member of a local Nez Perce' tribe. His name was *ESPOWYES*, which means "Light on the Mountain", but everyone called him Mountain instead. His tools were few, however they was all he owned, so now he was depressed. He had used the small bowl a few times with no results but, he knew there was gold in this spot. He had been find-ing some the day before. But, the thieves had also taken his poke or small bag of what he had gleaned so far.

He had watched the miners who had come to the mountains once word got out that John Sutter had found gold in his stream where they were building a new mill. So far, it was only local people showing up to stake a claim on any of the subsidiary streams in the area, but gold was being found everywhere they looked. Some of the white men wanted to increase their claims, so they hired some of Mountain's people to mine the claims for them, but they only paid them a few pennies a day for a full day of hard labor. Most of his people had no idea what the yellow rock was worth, but Mountain did.

He had been at the store near Sutter's when men came in and used the gold they had found to buy all sorts of things, including food and clothing. Things that his people would never be able to buy on the few pennies a day they earned from the miners. He was patient and waited, so that he could talk with the owner. After the men had left the store, he asked Mr. Sutter some questions. He had been patiently standing at the counter until finally Sutter noticed him.

"So now, young'un, what can I do fer you? Are ya here to buy something fer your miner?" said, Mr. Sutter.

"No sir. I want know, can I also find yellow rock in stream for myself?" said, Mountain.

"Well, I don't see why not. There ain't no law agin it. So you want to strike out on your own do ya?" said Mr. Sutter.

"When I find yellow rock, I can bring here to buy things?" asked Mountain.

"You sure can, boy. I reckon you might do well at that. You're gonna need some things, though. You might as well start with panning for it. For that you will need a large shallow bowl or pan," said Mr. Sutter.

"How much this?" asked the boy.

Mr. Sutter looked at Mountain with discerning eyes.

"I don't suppose you have even a penny on ya, do ya boy? Well, I have a proposition for ya. If you come here in the mornin' and do some work here in the store for me, for a couple of days, I will give you a pan and maybe a couple of other things you'll need. Heck, I didn't ask any of these fellers to come here and invade my land, but they keep on acomin' anyways. So I may as well let you be the first to get my personal permission to mine in my streams. Is that a deal, boy?" said Mr. Sutter, with a smile.

Mountain could not believe the generous offer. He stood dumbfounded and then finally nodded his head and hurried out of the store. The day was bright and sunny, the air fresh and clean, and he was certain that this time he would succeed.

One of Mr. Sutter's customers came through the open door just then.

"Now why'd you have to go and do that fer? Them injuns don't understand anythin' about gold and we don't need them to figger it out neither. Heck, if they knew they would probably not work for any of us agin'," said the miner.

"You just stay outta my business mister. I help who I want to and besides, I don't recollect you ever askin' to mine on my property. If'n I take a wild notion, I might come down the stream and shoo you all outta here with my scatter gun. So, keep your comments to your own self," said Mr. Sutter, now red from the neck up.

Mountain was on his way back to his village to let his mother know where he would be for the next few days. And that is how it had begun. While working at the store, he had watched the various purchases and how just a pinch of the yellow rocks would pay for many things. He quickly understood that his people were being taken advantage of by the miners. But, when he told the elders of his village what he had learned, they did not believe him. They could not conceive of any rock, no matter what color, that would be worth that much. They assumed that white men must want the rocks for some spiritual purpose or they were crazy.

So Mountain decided to keep his knowledge to himself and when he bought the many things at the store with a small amount of his yellow rocks, he would make believers of all the elders.

But, today he sat dejectedly by the part of the stream that Sutter said would be his to mine. Sutter had called it a "claim". He thought over what he should do next. He would have to start over; there was no question about that.

The next day he found himself back at Sutter's store. He waited for all the customers to leave before he approached Mr. Sutter.

"What now boy? Aren't ya havin' any luck?" asked Mr. Sutter.

"People came at night, toke my pan, my poke. I have no more yellow rock to buy with," said Mountain.

"Don't that beat all? Maybe I did not teach you enough before sending you out to mine your claim. First of all you have to find a hidin' place for your poke. You must hide it every day. It must be in a place that can't be washed out if the stream rises. Also, you need to keep your equipment with you where you sleep. That way you will wake up if someone tries to slip away with it. You're gonna have to be a mite more cautious if you expect to succeed in pannin' for gold.

"So I suppose you are lookin' to earn another pan and poke bag. Well, as it happens, I could use a little more help at the store. So come on back in the mornin' and let's be earnin' you some equipment," said Mr. Sutter.

Mr. Sutter watched as a smile grew across Mountain's face and he felt good, that this boy had not given up.

Mountain started for home, happy that Mr. Sutter needed more help. He would be back mining very soon.

He took the trail that lead to his village. The trail wound around the bluffs and small hills and crossed a couple of small streams. He came upon the first one and began to cross when he heard shouting. Not sure if he was in danger, he ran and hid behind some rocks on the other side of the stream and watched through the branches of a thicket. What he saw made his blood run cold.

Mountain's uncle was standing by the stream with a white man who was yelling and waving his arms around. Then the white man struck his uncle. His uncle stumbled back but did not retaliate. It was well known that Indians that hurt white men would be killed, no matter the reason.

"I don't want you to stop your pannin' for any reason, see? I say when you get to stop. I don't want no more, lazy, loafin' around. You're working for me now. So get to it," yelled the white man.

The boy watched while his uncle picked up the pan and began again to scoop up the under-water gravel and started to swirl the mass around until the yellow flakes and nuggets ended up at the bottom of the pan. The young boy saw no reason why his uncle had to demean himself to work for this white man who beat his workers.

As he continued down the trail, he debated in his mind whether or not he should tell his family about the incident. His uncle might not appreciate anyone knowing that he had let a white man strike him. However, he thought it would be better to show his people by using the gold rock to buy things his family needed. Then his uncle could quit working for the miner and mine the yellow rock for himself.

Mountain had worked three full days to earn back his equipment, with a few coins left over. So he quickly made his way back to his small claim. Once there he went about the chore of setting up camp again. By early afternoon,

Mountain was again panning for the gold rocks. He worked steadily for another five days, making sure to hide his poke each day and sleeping with his panning equipment.

On the sixth day, Mountain woke to find men standing over him and he sat up with a start.

"Well, lookee here, boys. We got us an injun who thinks he can pan for the gold his-self. I don't reckon he understands the way of things. Maybe we ought to enlighten him," said the one that was nearest to Mountain.

The man was very tall and wore a scruffy beard. The others with him, all solemn, dirty faced, white men, nodded their heads.

"This is my own claim. Mr. Sutter owns this land. He wrote claim down on your talking leaves that says this place I work is for me," said Mountain, his anger beginning to boil.

"Now, I don't see no paper here saying you have any rights. In fact injuns don't have no rights," said the tall one.

These words made no sense to Mountain.

"There are all these streams that have not been claimed yet. Mr. Sutter says, many will come to claim them soon. You can make a claim, anywhere, where there is no other claim. My claim is down in Mr. Sutter's writing. You cannot take my claim as long as I am working it," said the boy, trying to state the obvious.

But, Mountain did not understand the hate and prejudice that drove men to do unspeakable things. Even though the newcomers had their choice of thousands of sites where they could stake a claim, they seemed bent on causing him trouble.

"Ah, you see. That rule says you have to be working your claim. Boys, I think we can fix this here problem. Gold is for white men to mine, not injuns. So you better skedaddle on back to wherever you came from afore something happens to you," threatened the tall one.

Mountain did not move. He knew he had the right to work here and he had already worked at Sutter's store many days to buy back his equipment. He decided to not move or say anything more.

"Well, that's too bad. I really hate to disillusion you boy, but we is gonna head over to Sutter's to stake our claims and when we come back this way, you better be gone. If you ain't, then you won't be around to legally stake a claim to nothing in this world. You savvy me, boy?" said the tall one.

Mountain watched as they walked away. He had the idea that the threat was real, but he just could not give up on his claim. He worked for several more hours having some success and adding new nuggets to his poke. Suddenly, he heard voices. He sprang up from the gravel bar where he was panning, carrying his pan with him, and quickly he dashed into the woods behind him. He lay low, watching the men as they approached. He was thankful he had brought his pan and his poke with him.

The men stood around the camp looking every which way for the boy, but found no sign of him. The men had no tracking skills to speak of or they could have tracked him into the woods. Instead, they just let their eyes do the searching.

"Jeb, we need to be getting on down to our own claims afore someone tries to jump them," said one of the men to the tall one.

"Well, maybe that boy listened to us. Just the same, I'm gonna keep an eye open for him from time to time and if I find him here again, there will be one less injun in the world. We don't need to share any of the gold with no injuns," said Jeb, the tall one.

The men walked on down the stream while Mountain lay there shivering from fright. It was hard to know what to do. But for now, he would wait for them to leave and once gone, he would work until dark. Mountain figured he would find a more hidden place to sleep at night. He would work his claim regardless of the threat, but he would be ever vigilant to watch out for any white men coming along the stream in either direction. He knew his life could be at stake, but he wanted to prove to his family that they could use the gold rocks to help the People.

Three weeks later, Mr. Sutter was walking along the stream that led to his mill, and saw something floating in the swift current. He quickly stepped into the stream and grabbing the corner of a piece of leather, he pulled the object to shore. To his dismay, he recognized Mountain's clothing and realized that Mountain was still wearing them. He had been battered and bludgeoned to death. Mr. Sutter felt an overwhelming depression and anger as he looked down at the sad sight of the boy he tried to help.

Instinctively, he knew that worse times were ahead and he had no power to stop what was coming from happening. Everything he had worked for was in peril. But, where gold was concerned, men became crazed; laws and rules meant nothing anymore.

Mr. Sutter called for one of his hired hands, one of the few that still worked for him and had not gone out panning for gold. He arranged for them to go to the nearby Nez Perce' village so that Mountain's family could take care of the boy's body.

What else lay ahead in the months to come was unknown, but Mr. Sutter felt his future spinning out of his hands and he was greatly upset.

Chapter 1

The blustery day was ice cold, with gusts of wind, sending chilling fingers through cracks and crevices in the poorly built huts, freezing the skin under too thin coats and hatless heads in the Indian Territory. Winter was the hardest of the seasons for those living there, especially if the harvest did not go well the previous fall. People tending to outside chores or visiting neighbors plodded along on foot, if they had no horse, or rode a buckboard, a type of wagon, that gave little in the way of comfort.

Nothing about the last year had been easy. The tribes kept vigil on their crops and livestock, but saw little hope of regaining the prosperity and wealth they had possessed in their homelands from which they had been removed in 1838-39. Almost ten years later it seemed little progress had been accomplished and the only people they could rely on were themselves. There were a select few who had brought their wealth with them and were doing well, but that was not the majority.

The tribe that left the most wealth behind was the Cherokee, and it was difficult to say if they would ever get back what they had lost back in Georgia, Tennessee, or North and South Carolina. Some, because of foresight and knowledge, were able to transfer their wealth to Indian Territory, and so lived a somewhat gentler life than most. But the vast majority of the tribe still worked from sun up to sun down, striving to make a new life in a harsh new land.

Willa Halley, the adopted daughter of Anna and Jackson Halley, was not unaware of the struggles in Indian Territory, but her new parents had taken good care of her and so she was somewhat shielded from the wave of hate and violence that was growing in the territory. At the time, the Halley's adopted Willa, they also adopted Charlie, also a Cherokee, and baby Emma, a Choctaw, all rescued from the child stealers that occasionally swept the territory looking for unattended children to abduct and sell in the states. Willa's grandmother had given her up willingly to one of these men, with the promise that she would be raised well. But, it had been a lie. Willa's grandmother knew her time was limited and having no other family, saw no other way to make sure Willa would be looked after. Willa's grandmother died last year. Now, she had no family in Indian Territory or within her Cherokee Nation.

Willa sat on Sasa's lap in their comfortable rocking chair, which was in the living room of the Halley's home and mule breeding ranch. Sasa, the Halley's other adopted Cherokee daughter and Willa's constant companion, sat beside her gently rocking, while looking out of the front window at the trees being buffeted by the icy breeze. Sasa's marriage to Coyote, the man from the Lakota tribe to the far north west, limited the time in which she could spend with her adopted sister, but today, Sasa made time.

In the years, after removal, the Cherokee had experienced much trouble and divisiveness. The elders, who had illegally signed the treaty allowing for the removal of the entire tribe, found that they were the targets of a blood feud. It had been agreed long before that any Cherokee selling or giving his land to the whites without consent from the tribe, would be subject to a sentence of death. And so it happened that several of the treaty signers had been murdered. Some, like Stand Watie, one of the treaty signers, escaped this murderous rampage by being forewarned. However, Stand and his "Treaty Party" followers retaliated, resulting in years of blood feud within the tribe. Murder had become so prevalent that news of a new victim would be met with a shrug. There did not seem to be a way to end the feud, so most went on about the business of making their farms and livestock produce.

"How long can you stay Sasa?" asked Willa.

"Only a little while longer dear, Coyote will be here soon. We have some errands to run in town and we want to get back home before dark. Let us just enjoy the time we have together now. There will always be other days, I assure you," said Sasa, with a slight smile on her lovely Cherokee face.

Sasa stroked Willa's long black hair as they rocked back and forth. Willa felt extremely content whenever she was with Sasa. Now seven years old, Willa could barely remember when she lived in the Territory. She knew that was where her family had lived and that the Cherokee Nation was there, centered around Tahlequah. But, she felt somewhat removed from it all.

Sasa took it upon herself to teach Willa as much about the Cherokee as she had time for. However, her marriage to Coyote prevented her from spending all the time she would have liked. Even though Coyote put no real constraints on her time, she felt it her duty to be as good a wife as she could be.

Coyote had made many changes in his life since he left his Lakota people to the north. He now spoke English fluently and also some Cherokee as well. He earned his living there at Halley's Mule Breeding Ranch and seemed to enjoy his work.

Sasa and Coyote live in a small, neat cottage Jackson had built for them as a wedding gift. It was only a few hundred yards to the west of the ranch, nestled in a cozy meadow, giving it a feeling of privacy. Sasa was very happy with her home; however, she still built a traditional brush arbor in the front yard, so they could sit in the shade of it and enjoy the outdoors together, weather permitting. Today was not one of those days.

As they sat slowly rocking, Sasa felt a slight push at her side. She looked down to see Wheezer, Jackson's Jack Russell Terrier, stretching his legs against her side, rumpling her calico dress. She smiled at him and patted him on the head. Wheezer was an unusual dog. He was so smart, that many people felt that he could understand their every word. There was no doubt that he understood much of what was being said, because Wheezer had saved Sasa's life more than once with just a word from Jackson. Sasa and Wheezer were inseparable, ever since the day Sasa rescued him from certain death next to a creek in the forest.

Wheezer also had a mate. Her name was Penny and she had produced several good litters of Jack Russell pups for the ranch. Rev. John Russell, who spent many years perfecting the breed, gave both Wheezer and Penny to Jackson. Wheezer was the first of this new breed to cross the ocean to America. Later Rev. Russell sent Penny over so that Jackson would have a good pair for mating. The Halley family had experienced many hours of entertainment and fun, due to the good nature of the Jack Russell Terriers. In addition to that, Wheezer had become a life-long friend and companion to Sasa. His intelligence, courage and quick action had saved the lives of many people in the past. Penny, on the other hand, preferred to stay at the side of Jackson at the ranch.

Sasa continued to ponder over the cold and blustery day, dreading the trip into town, but it could not be avoided. At least, they did not have to cross the Arkansas River to Fort Smith on the army ferry. Van Buren, Arkansas, the town closest to the ranch, was finally getting some good businesses, resulting in the expansion of the town and providing many families with needed supplies. Fort Smith used to be the only place to find those needed supplies and it still was the main supplier of goods for most of Indian Territory, just to the west of Van Buren. The fort was still active at Fort Smith and remained one of the biggest customers for Halley's Mule Breeding Ranch. The fort preferred mules instead of horses for their mounts, because of their stamina and ruggedness.

It was hard to tell the time of day from the light outside the window. Heavy cloud cover, kept the light dim. It looked like it could be late afternoon, when it truth, the clock chimed ten in the morning just a moment before. The pale light through the window settled on her dress, but there was not enough light to show off the pretty blues, reds and greens in her traditional Cherokee Tear Dress. As Sasa contemplated the weather outside, Anna, Jackson's wife, stepped into the front room of the ranch house with Emma tottering by her side. Anna was the stepmother of Willa, Charlie and baby Emma, as Jackson's first wife had died. Emma was a shy child of almost four, who stuck by Anna's side throughout the day. So far, Anna had not been able to conceive a child of her own, but she found that her three stepchildren satisfied that need nicely.

"Has Jackson come in from the corral yet?" asked Anna.

Sasa stretched up her arms and yawned, "No, but I expect him any time now. You can't do much out there in this kind of weather. Also, he knows Coyote and I must go for supplies in town soon, and that will take the rest of the day, I am sorry to say," said Sasa.

"Well, I know Jackson thinks Charlie is almost an adult, and can work like all the other ranch hands, but just because he is getting taller and appears older, he is still a child and should not have to work out in this terrible weather. I don't want him catching his death from a cold or worse. If he doesn't let him come in soon, I will go and get him myself," said Anna, in a matter of fact way.

"No need to worry Anna, Charlie and Jackson will be in soon. Charlie has only been out barely over an hour. I think he is big enough to take it. But, he will be cold when he gets in, so I better stoke up the fire before they arrive," said Sasa.

She suited her actions to her words, and rose to build up the fire in the grate with a couple more logs. Which caused Wheezer to, jump down from the rocker and give a good shake of his white and brown fur. Willa also stood and retrieved her cloth doll from the window seat.

"Willa, you did not make your bed this morning. Please go and do it now before Papa Jackson gets back," said Anna.

Willa pulled a face and went to her room, not liking the task at all. Keeping their rooms tidy was one of the few chores Anna required of the children, and for the most part, they obeyed without complaint.

Sasa, now standing by the front window, watched for any sign that the men were coming back. Her thoughts began to wander back to the days of her schooling, provided by Jackson at much cost. The hours and hours of tutoring by the Professor of Law, whom Jackson had hired, were sometimes brutal, but she had been determined to learn. Learning the law of the white man was the key to helping her people, which they still needed desperately. Every month, she traveled into Indian Territory to the capitol of the Cherokee Nation, Tahlequah, and helped families with legal questions. She could never be a lawyer since she was a woman and an Indian, but she could direct people to the right places, to get the help they needed.

Sometimes, they only needed reassurance, as in the case of the continuing battle over the money due the Cherokee from the U.S. Government. There was nothing they could do except be patient, while Chief Ross continued to fight for what was promised. Some just needed her to translate a legal document from English to Cherokee, since many residents still did not read English.

Even though the Indian Territory tribes maintained their own laws, white man's laws applied to them whenever they ventured out of the territory. So, Sasa made herself available, to answer any questions the Cherokee individuals and families wanted to know. In a few cases, she had been invited to attend tribal councils, as an observer, so that she could explain the decisions to any that needed an explanation. She found her role fulfilling. She felt she had a purpose and that she was needed.

Now, problems in the territory had escalated to a point where it was dangerous to travel alone without protection. Sasa was thankful she had Coyote now. Ever since their marriage, she was happy to rely on him for protection. He was brave, courageous and clever. In the few times he had been involved in a fight, he had always come out as the winner. His strength was not just in his body, but in his mind as well. In a very short time he had mastered English and was very close to mastering Cherokee as well. He could so easily be arrogant and selfish; instead he was kind and thoughtful. Sasa loved Coyote very much.

However, lately Sasa had noticed a restlessness in Coyote. He was still a young man, and very probably craved a young man's adventures. It was his choice to settle down with Sasa. She in no way enticed him into marriage; however she sometimes caught a faraway look in his eyes and wistfulness in his manner. It would be natural to a young man his age, to yearn for adventure and excitement, to see new places and experience new things. Sasa thought about it from time to time, but she could not come up with a solution that would keep Coyote by her side, and at the same time give him what he obviously longed for. There were very little opportunities outside of Indian Territory for an Indian of any tribe, so her choices at the moment, were slim to none.

She pushed the thought out of her head, as she saw him walking with Jackson and Charlie, from the corral. No doubt they would be cold and ready for some hot coffee, to say the least. She never tired of admiring his physic, as she watched him walk towards the house. He was dressed in buckskins and a coat of wolf and badger pelts. His hair was black, straight and pulled to a queue behind his head. He wore no hat or gloves and always seemed to be at home, in whatever weather he found himself.

He had the customary high cheekbones and straight nose of the Lakota tribe and the height of the Northern

Blackfoot tribe. He had never been accepted well in his mother's Lakota camp, because he was half Northern Blackfoot, traditional enemies of the Lakota. His mother had been taken in a raid, and forced into marriage with a Blackfoot warrior. But, when the warrior proved to be a bad provider, she had the right to divorce him and soon left the Blackfoot camp to return to her Lakota home. Only by then, she was pregnant by the hated Blackfoot warrior and her resulting son bore the brunt of that, as he grew up.

The Lakota were constantly at war with one tribe or another, but Coyote was more interested in healing. He learned the craft at the feet of the tribe's medicine man. Rather than be forced to participate in endless raids, he chose to leave and seek out a new life. He traveled south and eventually into Indian Territory at about the same time that the last of the Cherokee groups made it to their new homeland. The Cherokee forced removal from the east, had become known as "The Trail of Tears", and for good reason. Thousands had died on that long trek and once the Cherokee were there, they suffered even further hardships, including starvation.

Sasa watched as the group mounted the front porch steps with obvious anticipation of the warmth to be found inside the house. Charlie entered first, before the men, while Coyote let Jackson go in ahead of him, so that he could secure the front door.

"Too cold to do any training today," said Jackson.

Anna just nodded then called for Masey, their cook and housekeeper, to set the dining room table for coffee and cake. It was yet too early for lunch. Wheezer, though, was already in his chair at the table, waiting for them all to sit. Sasa had suggested that Wheezer be given a chair at the table, if he behaved himself and Wheezer seemed to understand the rules. He never put a paw on the table and waited patiently for Jackson or Anna to give him his portion. It was a bit eccentric, indeed, to treat an animal in such a way, but Wheezer had become a part of their family. After saving several children, in an upstairs Fort Smith room, from certain death, the Halley family decided to indulge him at their table. So far Wheezer remained a complete gentleman.

Before they could all sit themselves at the table, a sharp knock at the door caused Wheezer to grumble his impatience. Sasa hurried to open the door, as soon as it was opened, a young Cherokee man came in quickly, closing the door behind him.

"Samuel, what are you doing out on a day like today? The ride over here must have frozen you stiff," said Jackson, with a small shiver.

Samuel was a neighbor who sometimes worked on the ranch with Jackson and his crew. He regarded the Halley's ranch as a home away from home.

"Have y'all read the Fort Smith paper today? There is busting news and I just had to come over and tell ya," said Samuel, breathlessly.

"Masey, bring another chair out for our guest. Also, we'll need another place setting," said Jackson.

Masey disappeared into the kitchen to obey, muttering under her breath and her gray stiff dress, swishing through the doorway.

"Well, take your coat off and get warm, Samuel," said Jackson.

Samuel pulled a face, as if waiting would cause him some kind of pain. But, he complied without verbal complaint and took the seat offered to him. Wheezer began to shake with anticipation, of the food to come and looked puzzled as to why everyone was still standing.

"Please, let us all sit down and then you can tell us your news," said Anna.

After they settled in their chairs, Samuel pulled from his pocket an article he had cut out of the newspaper. His hands were trembling with excitement and his eyes sparkled with fervor.

"What is it you bring to us today, Samuel," said Jackson.

"I found this here article in the Arkansas Intelligencer. It is a reprint from October 6, 1848. It is dated January 8, 1949. I am afraid it is already several days old. It is entitled, "California Gold". Jackson, would you read it? I am not that good at reading out loud," said Samuel.

"Alright, I will read it while Anna pours the coffee," said Jackson, a little dubious of the importance of the news. Information about gold being found anywhere, seemed like pie in the sky to him.

He began to read and all ears were quickly attuned and curious.

"It begins, "California Gold", then goes on...

We have received through the New Orleans papers... such accounts from California, as leave little doubt, that the stories of the mineral wealth of the country, however exaggerate, are founded in fact... a report derived from an officer of the Army, bearer of dispatches...gives the following: 'The News which these Gentlemen bring...fully confirms all the account...The whole valley of the Sacramento may be said to be one vast deposit of gold, the metal lying in more or less abundance, from the crags of the Sierra Nevada to the embouchures of that river, and its many tributaries. People were completely engrossed in collecting it, to the abandonment of almost every other occupation...

Many persons have collected, in one day, the finest grade gold, from three to eight hundred dollars, and for many days...averaged from 75 to $150... when a man with *his pan or basket does not easily gather 30 to 40 dollars in a day he moves to another place…we, may safely set down an ounce of pure Gold, or $16 per day to the man. Suppose there are 4,000 persons at work, they will add to the aggregate wealth of the Territory about 4,000 ounces, or $60,000 a day…'*

A letter in the National Intelligencer…contains the following eloquent language in relation to the yellow metal: 'The Shores are paved with it, and the Mountains swell in its Golden Girdle. It sparkles in the Sands of the Valley; It glitters in the Coronet of the Steep Cliffs…' I use strong terms but who can speak in whispers when an Earthquake rocks?

Samuel looked up at the end of Jackson's reading, impatient. "It has to be true. They wouldn't print somethin' like that if it ain't, would they, Jackson?"

"No, I don't suppose they would, Samuel," said Jackson.

"But that's not all," said Samuel, as he pulled another piece of paper out of his other pocket and passed it over to Jackson.

"I just tore this out of a friend's paper. It was in yesterday's Advocate dated January 22nd. Now you just go on ahead and read that there. Things are really happenin'," said Samuel, excitedly.

Jackson took the article, smoothing it out where it had gotten crumpled in Samuel's pocket and began to read.

"The title says, 'FOR CALIFORNIA', and it goes on to say:

'There is a company forming in Tahlequah, Cherokee Nation, for California - - with the design of joining the company now forming in Fort Smith, which company will leave the first of April. The regulations or the necessary equipments required by said company of each emigrant

are: a good rifle, plenty of ammunition, rations for the journey, consisting of 180 lbs of Flour and 100 lbs of Bacon, to be transported in wagons drawn by horses, mules or oxen.

All young men in the Nation, who may wish to try their fortunes in the Gold Regions of California, have now the opportunity. Any persons wishing further information with regard to the 'tramp' can obtain it by applying to the undersigned, Tahlequah, C. Nation.

JAS. S. VANN

DANL. M. GUNTER'"

Jackson took a deep breath and let the air out in a long whistle.

"That really is news," said Jackson, as he looked around the table at all who sat there staring at him wide eyed. "I am surprised that James Vann, the editor of the Cherokee Phoenix newspaper is advertising for a Cherokee Company to provide for the trip. I can see a multitude of problems with that. But, obviously he seems to be going ahead with his stated intentions," said Jackson. Anna and Sasa looked at each other with worried looks.

"Gold will make people crazy. Just like it did when we found gold on our land in Georgia," said Sasa. "The white men just came and took it all away and used a gun to hold them at bay. At least that is what my father told me. He had been there and witnessed it."

The others nodded around the table.

"This gold strike sounds big and keeping Indians away may not be an issue. There is no way to tell at this point in time," said Jackson.

"I see, they mention the need for mules. Do you think we have enough stock to supply the company, if they come to you?" said Anna, looking at Jackson with a wrinkled brow.

"No…No I don't, but I know where I can get more. I think we may have to sit down with Mr. Vann and see what he thinks will be the needs of this company, heading west. and then see if we can oblige them," said Jackson.

Samuel screwed up his face in bewilderment. "You don't understand, do you? It is not just the Cherokee company. This whole area is going to erupt with people from all over wantin' ta leave from Fort Smith. I heard tell, that Independence has so many people getting' ready to leave, that they couldn't find room for them all. There's fights and drunken brawls, shootins' and robbery in the camps and there abouts. And I even heard there is disease spreadin in those camps too. It's too early to leave because the grass ain't up yet, but they still keep on acommin'. Least ways, that's what Earl told me and he just came from there," said Samuel, trembling with excitement and anticipation.

Jackson opened his eyes wide and was silent for a few heartbeats. "You are right. I had not thought of that. We could be overrun with companies wanting to buy mules. I imagine that oxen will be the preferred animals for the trip, but they will still want mules as well. The companies will have to go south of Fort Smith to find oxen in any numbers. Now that you mention it, Samuel, I think we have no idea of what is going to fall on us here and soon! I think it might be best if we set up here in the dining room, this afternoon, and take stock of what we have and what we can get hold of on short notice," replied Jackson.

Suddenly, Wheezer began to whine and pat his front paw on the tabletop in front of him. Jackson smiled without a word and placed a small slice of cake on the plate in front of Wheezer. But, Wheezer did not eat. Instead, he gazed at Jackson intently waiting for permission.

"Wheezer, we have to say grace first. Remember? Bow your head," said Jackson.

Everyone, including Wheezer bowed their heads while Jackson said a short prayer for their food. Then Jackson chuckled under his breath and then nodded his head. Wheezer gingerly took a piece of his cake in his mouth and swallowed it down. He continued in that fashion, without gulping it down, until all his cake was eaten. This ritual was a daily routine for meals at the table, but it was new to Samuel who stared in disbelief at the dog.

"Well I never, how in tarnation did you teach him to do that? Most dogs would gulp it all down lickety-split and no bones about it," said Samuel.

Jackson, Anna and Sasa looked at each other with knowing smiles, while Coyote explained.

"Wheezer taught himself. He wants to be with us during meals and he knows he has to obey the rules. If he does not, then he has to have his cake in the kitchen on the floor and he will do anything to keep that from happening. So, he gets fed what we are having, except we don't give him coffee or wine. Wheezer just seems to know, that he must imitate the humans at the table," said Coyote, with a mischievous grin.

The group continued to talk about the news, until it was time for lunch to be served. Wheezer had gone back to the front room and curled up on the rocker, waiting for lunch. Samuel was invited to stay. Even after lunch, the group continued to mull over the news and plan on how best to meet the coming needs of the newly formed companies going west. Wheezer could sense the excitement and looked expectantly at Sasa, in case he might miss something fun.

"Settle down Wheezer. Nothing is happening right now. Don't worry; we won't forget to include you. Now why don't you go and play with Penny in the barn, I am sure she misses you," said Sasa, as she began to clear the table in case Jackson needed to use it for more planning.

Chapter 2

A few miles away in Washington County, Arkansas, Lewis Evans sat preparing his next advertisement to be placed in the Fort Smith Herald. He was recently voted Captain of the wagon train that would head for the gold fields in a few months time. Evans had founded a small town in Arkansas called Evansville, but Fort Smith was the closest town with a proper newspaper. However, many of the interested parties seemed to be coming from Fayetteville, Arkansas. Not to mention the surrounding counties as well. So Evans decided to call his company, The Fayetteville Gold Mining Company. His best friend and helper was David Newcomb; a brave Arkansas pioneer, who seldom got upset over small things.

"I just don't know if this is going to work out or not. We need more immigrants to make the trip for California, but at the same time, getting supplies is eventually going to become a problem," said Captain Evans, as he scratched his forehead.

"I say, write the invitation and let the immigrants worry about it. You don't know that some may have their own stock and grain. And there is plenty of time to gather what other things they need. Besides the fact, that some of them are coming from outside Arkansas and they have other sources for their supplies than we do. I also heard some are coming from as far away as Independence," said David, while he organized the names of those already confirmed for the trip.

"Independence? Why on earth would they come down here when the Santa Fe Trail begins there?" said Captain Evans.

Evans looked up from his writing, waiting for David to answer.

"I thought you knew. Disease has broken out in the camps up there. It is forcing many to find a new way. The word is just now reaching them that there are companies planning on taking the southern route. They will do anything to keep away from cholera and the other deadly diseases. They say there are already a number of dead in the camps," said David.

Traders like Josiah Gregg had used the southern route, for many years. In fact, Evans had written to Mr. Gregg asking for advice and instruction about the road and the Indians they might meet along the way. But, Evans was still a bit unsettled about taking that route. With the recent Indian uprisings, it may not be safe to travel that road. On the other hand, what other road was there? None he was aware of. He would have to continue planning on the southern route. You never knew when things and plans would change. It was a rough country, which could be deadly, if a man were unprepared. That was the reason for all the planning he was doing now.

The newly formed company had had a meeting, night before last, where Evans was elected Captain. There would not be another meeting for a month. Maybe by then, plans would be a little clearer. So he continued with his advertisement. It read:

A Company is now being formed at Fayetteville, Arkansas, consisting of vigorous, enterprising and substantial citizens of Washington and adjoining counties, with the intention of paying a visit to the gold mines of California and securing a portion of the rich deposits of that region. The Company will start from Fayetteville about the first of April and will pursue the most advantageous route. A committee has been appointed to collect all the facts that can be procured in relation to the several routes....

Evans sat back from his desk and pondered. Hopefully, by the next meeting, the committee would have more information about the best way to proceed.

*****

Deep in the forests south of Fayetteville, Arkansas resided a small community loosely spaced around the countryside. The families raised pigs, goats, cattle, and farmed what land they were able to clear sufficiently for the sun to reach the ground. It was not a good living, but it got the families by. Among them was a family man, Stan Grant. He worked hard for his wife Bessie and three children. The children, two boys and a girl, were of an age to be of help around the farm and that fact is what had been occupying Stan's mind for some time now. He had heard about the gold finds in California and was itching to make the trip himself. He wanted to give his wife and kids something better than the hand to mouth life he had given them so far. But, his wife would need the help of the children and none of them had the strength of a man.

The only way out of this problem was to ask his neighbor, Curtis Bledsoe, to look in on Bessie from time to time. He was not sure his neighbor would do it. Curtis had not been that friendly of a neighbor over the years, and he did not like the way Curtis looked at his Bessie. He knew Bessie was no shrinking violet. She could wield a frying pan if anyone got fresh. It just gave him pause, to leave her alone with only Curtis to look in on her.

He remembered when the Rev. Phineas Piney from the church in the next community down the road, stopped in to check on Stan's family. Rev. Piney was not too pleased about the idea of California gold and leaving the family behind.

"I don't think God cares too much for riches Stan. It is a wild goose chase and think of the danger of you, maybe not making it back to your wife and children. Is it not a bit selfish for you to force them to be without your protection, while you chase your rainbow of gold?" said Rev. Piney.

The Reverend had stood in the middle of the front room, close to the big fire in the fireplace, blocking its heat. His black coat and trousers were worn and almost threadbare, but he seemed not to notice his appearance. He wore a very wide brimmed hat that shaded his face and he always seemed to hold a handkerchief up to his mouth claiming he had a cold, although, Stan had never heard him cough.

"No Rev. Piney, I don't think it is selfish. My family is the reason why I am going. It is the quickest way for us to get a leg up. Lots of people are going, are you saying they are all just being greedy?" asked Stan.

"Not greedy, but certainly foolhardy," said Rev. Piney.

"Well, if you were in the same position as I am now, you might think twice about it. The reports say, that the gold is just laying on top of the ground. And even if I had to dig for it, it would be worth the work. My family needs things I can't provide and I think I would be a fool to not go. Really Reverend, you need to think on it yourself," said Stan.

The Reverend just shook his head and then placing his handkerchief in his pocket, walked down the path to the next family.

At the moment, Stan was in the barn, taking stock of the supplies he thought he would need for the trip. It was a hard winter and the ground was frozen, so he could not prepare any of his fields, ahead of time, to help his wife.

His wagon stood silent next to him, waiting for the day he would hook up the two span of oxen. That would leave Bessie, two oxen and two mules for the plowing and stump pulling on the farm. He had saved half of his harvest of wheat for flour and had just gotten the bags back from the mill. He was all ready to go. He would take, twenty of the fifteen pound slabs of bacon he had hanging in the smoke house and leave the rest for her. He took salt, sugar, baking soda, coffee and other odds and ends he thought would come in handy. He wanted to take the milk cow, but they only possessed one and he had to leave it at home. Maybe he could buy milk from another traveler. However, he did have several rounds of home made cheese in potato sacks. Hopefully, it would last all the way to California.

He had also taken several different kinds of tools, extra spokes for the wheels and an extra wagon wheel. He tried to be prepared for any sort of mishaps. But, being cautious caused his load to be heavy and he would just have to just make do with the oxen he could pull away from the farm.

Bessie was in the house baking bread. She would wrap it up in paper and it would last several days, before he would have to start making biscuits for him-self. In a wooden box he carried the ammunition for his rifle. It was a Hawken, new in 1840, out of St. Louis, Missouri, and the pride of his gun collection. He would have to leave the shotgun and most of his pistols here with Bessie. But, she knew how to use them, of that he was totally sure. Even though he did not totally trust Curtis Bledsoe, at least there was some help close by if Bessie absolutely needed it. At least, that is what he told himself.

As Stan continued to pack the wagon with supplies, he noticed a figure walking over the fields towards his barn. He did not have to wonder who it was, since there was not another man in the area other than Curtis Bledsoe. And indeed, it was he. Curtis came huffing and puffing in the bitter cold air, and stopped just inside the barn door.

"Ah, I see you are almost ready to take off," said Curtis.

"Next few days, I think will do it. Not really sure how much of this to take or what might be available in Fort Smith. But it is better to be prepared. I can always sell off anything I don't need later," said Stan.

Curtis took a few moments to look over the stacks of boxes and canvas bags of supplies. He licked his lips as if he were about to eat a meal.

"How much do you think it has cost ya to gather all this stuff?" asked Curtis.

"Don't rightly know, Curtis. I've been saving up in case I had a bad year, ever since I married Bessie. So it'll come in handy. And, onest I found out about the gold strike in Cal-iforn-I-A, I thought it would help me make this trip. Now, I'm tryin' to decide what to take of the food stores. Don't want Bessie and the kids to suffer any, no how. I imagine there will be opportunity to kill a few buffalo out on the prairie. So, that oughta help me out some. What about you? You still plannin' on stayin' to home?" said Stan.

Curtis looked indecisive for a moment, scratched his head and shook it slowly as if to relieve it of a bad thought.

"No, I can't make the trip. No supplies. You sure you don't want a partner to go with ya? I don't have much to add to the stores, but I sure as heck would like to go," said Curtis.

"Sorry Curtis, but I don't have enough food stuffs for two. It just wouldn't work out, is all. I'd like the company, but I can't see a way ifin' you don't have your own food to bring with ya," said Stan.

Curtis put a sour look on his face for a brief moment before Stan looked back at him, he was all smiles.

They said their good-byes and Stan watched as a dejected Curtis trudged back to his shack over the next field. He wondered a moment about it and then put it out of his mind, intent on his chore.

That night, a tired Stan sat at the table mentally checking off the list of supplies he had packed that day. He was almost ready to go. Just a few clothes and some extra feed for the oxen, because the grass was not yet up. Bessie came over and refilled his cup of hot steaming coffee. As she set the pot back on the stove, she decided to have a small talk with Stan.

"Darlin', you know I would never stand in your way of goin', but I am just a mite worried about how we will fair without ya. I don't like to have to ask Curtis. Sides, he has no reason to spend much time helpin' a family that ain't his. But, ifin' your set on goin', I spose you oughta have my love to take with ya. That's all I gotta say on that, ceptin' I expect you ta come home quick as ya can. Don't stay out there and get all the gold! We don't need much. Just go get some and leave the rest for others and come on home," said Bessie.

Stan barely heard her speech. He was so busy with the figures in his head, her words did not penetrate. He nodded absentmindedly. Bessie sighed, knowing her plea had gone unheard. She could only hope common sense would win out. Her Stan was not prone to flights of fancy, so she had to trust in him. She could do all the plowing and planting, and the children would help with all the other chores. She had done it before when Stan fell ill one year. But, she would be very lonely. She had family back in Virginia, however, that was a very long way from Arkansas. She would just have to do the best she could. What else was there to do?

Chapter 3

Stan drove his oxen up a long grade headed for the road that would take him to Fort Smith. He had a long way to go yet; he had only been on the road an hour or so. The path he followed was not so bad, but the trees alongside hung down low and brushed the top of his top sheet over the wagon. Hopefully the branches would not cause a rip. That was the only thing protecting his provisions inside, if it rained. Various things he had tied to the sides of the wagon, like rope, the water barrel, and extra chains. Various tools clanked as the wagon jerked along. But, the sound was not bothering Stan. It seemed to add to his excitement, knowing that he was really on his way.

He wore dungarees, a plaid flannel shirt and a leather topcoat over that. The air was still cold, but the sun was shining down mightily. Stan smiled as he remembered Bessie's farewell kiss. It was going to have to last him for some time to come. But, it was a doozy. Up ahead he noticed some heavy branches lying across the path that led up and over the hill. A storm or heavy wind must have downed them in the last storm. He slowed the team until he was just a few yards from the blockage, grabbed his hand axe, set the break on the wheels and jumped down to remove it.

He worked for some time, clearing away the debris and was almost ready to get on down the road when a sharp crack echoed through the hills. Stan was unaware for a moment that he had been hurt, but very soon he felt the sting of it in his chest. He fell to the ground, still wondering what had happened, when a man climbed down from the tree beside the path. The man had a woman's stocking pulled over his face with cut out holes for his eyes. Stan was having a hard time, thinking, his mind was racing, worrying about Bessie and his children. How could this happen? Who was this person and why did he shoot him? But, the man did not speak.

The man stood in the path waiting, but for what, Stan was unsure. Then it dawned on him that the man was after his wagon and supplies. He knew he would be a dead man for sure if he did not do something to prevent it and he was helpless to fight back. He quickly remembered what the animals looked like when he went hunting and had shot one dead. The eyes would be open and stare ahead, unblinking. Could he do that? Could he keep this man from finishing him off?

Soon, Stan slumped back onto the ground, opened his eyes and stared fixedly. He could hear the man chuckle. Before he knew what was happening, the man grabbed hold of the neck of Stan's jacket and pulled him off of the path. Stan continued to stare, not blinking or moving a twitch. He could feel the blood leaking out of his chest and soaking his shirt. The icy winds bit into him as he lay on the frozen ground.

Stan could hear the man grunting with sounds of scraping. He was probably clearing the rest of the limbs from the path. The man finally came back to Stan's body looking closely at him, and then viciously kicking him in the back. It took all of Stan's will not to grunt or move. Soon he could hear his wagon pulling away from his body. He was being left for dead. Maybe he really was going to be dead anyway, since he was a long way from home. How far would he get with a wound in his chest? Slowly, he raised his head and looked at the last view of the wagon he would ever see. Now he had to find a way to get help.

With excruciating pain, he made it up on his hands and knees. He took several deep breaths before trying to stand. Slowly, one step at a time he stumbled down the path the way he had come. Unknowing whether each step would be his last, he kept going, as long as what little strength he had left held out. He was still stumbling along when he noticed the sun was beginning to descend. Had he really been at this all day long?

The bitter cold deepened and showed no signs of letting up. The cold was as deadly as the hole in his chest. Then, just as dusk was settling on the earth around him, a wagon appeared on the path ahead of him. He had no idea who it might be, but he knew he had to get help, for if he stayed in the forest overnight, apart from bleeding to death, the wolves and coyotes would be glad to feed on him and he would be frozen by morning. The wagon pulled alongside. Stan noticed it carried a mound of last year's hay.

"Here now, what had happened to ya young feller?" asked the man in the wagon.

Stan could barely speak, but tried to explain.

"Wagon stolen – shot - left for dead. Name - Stan Grant - over Fair Grove way. Help me!" said Stan as his knees buckled under him and he slumped down to the ground.

The man in the wagon was astonished. This kind of thing just did not happen in these parts. People here about were honest and hard working. Fair Grove was not very far away; it was just a tiny community, barely five families in all. But his first order of business would be to get this young man to the closest doctor or he was dead for sure. The man got down from his wagon and with pushing and pulling, got Stan up in the wagon on the soft hay. He headed for Fayetteville where he knew there was help.

*****

Willie Catcher had walked the Trail of Tears with his Cherokee brothers and sisters, losing his wife to cold and disease along the way. The loss of his beautiful wife and the fact he had had to leave her in a shallow grave along side the road made every mile away from her a torture. Each step he took along the trail was agonizing. He had started out with a good pair of moccasins, but after the first one hundred miles, they fell apart quite literally as he walked. He had wrapped his feet in rags, which were constantly coming undone, but it saved his feet from frostbite. Many of the Cherokee on the trail had lost one or several toes to the freezing temperatures, with no shoes to speak of.

After arriving in Indian Territory, he staked his claim to a portion of land a few miles outside of Tahlequah, intending on producing crops. But the crops were meager at best. He lacked the necessary equipment to work the majority of his land, so every year many acres lay fallow. He lacked the animals that could have grazed on that land. He did have two span of oxen and two tough mules. It was

27

enough to help him plow his crops, but no helpers, slaves or otherwise. Many of the Cherokees owned slaves they had brought with them from the east. Willie had never had the funds to acquire such a luxury.

He was blessed, though, in one way, in that he had found a new wife to share his meager living. He had built for her a log home like the one he had had in the East. She kept it warm and clean. They were expecting their firstborn in just a few months and the thought of that kept Willie's spirits high. Except, when he thought of how close his family lived to poverty, causing him much shame and distress.

That is why when he saw the advertisement in the Advocate of February 12, the one inviting men to join a company of immigrants to travel to the gold mines recently discovered in California, he began to spend his day dreaming of the possibilities. He had told his wife, Clara, about the gold and what it could mean to them, but she was strangely silent and grim. He took little notice of her silence. Each day he would mentally work out the problems of acquiring the provisions for the trip. He would probably have to borrow, even beg for them. He had little to trade, except for his land and he was determined to not let go of it.

Little by little, Willie acquired the bare necessities for the trip as outlined in the recent letter in the paper. He had torn out the article and kept it folded in his pocket for easy access. It was well worn, for whenever he took a break; he would pull it out and reread it with relish.

"WHEREAS, the intelligence which has reached us of the California gold mines, is corroborated by official reports, which render it certain that there is sufficient for all who wish to avail themselves of the opportunity of improving their fortunes.

---And whereas it is imperatively necessary that persons going should form themselves into a company, and remain united through the journey in order to repel

attacks, to afford mutual succor, and ensure success of the enterprise, therefore, we a portion of the Cherokee People, designing to avail ourselves of the inducements held out for bettering our condition by emigrating thither, and wishing to organize ourselves into a company to proceed in such a manner as shall ensure our safety, our comfort, and success, do resolve,

1st. That it would be neither safe, nor expedient, to proceed with less than 100 able bodied efficient men, well armed with a rifle gun, a butcher knife, and sufficient ammunition to last through the journey, say, not less then 3 lbs of powder, and 9 lbs of lead.

Resolved 2nd. That each man shall furnish provisions sufficient to support him during the journey, not less than 100 lbs of bacon, 200 lbs of flour, 25 lbs salt and 2 lbs soap.

Resolved 3rd. That each wagon shall not be drawn by less than one yoke of cattle or mules to each ration, that each wagon be furnished with six gallons of tar, and not less than one axe, one handsaw, one drawing knife and one set of necessary augers and chisels.

Resolved 4th. That no wagons carry more than 20 cwt., and small ones less in proportion, which is to be determined by a committee.

Resolved 5th. That the company rendezvous by the 1st day of April at Richard Drew's, on the south side of Arkansas River, where all necessary officers are to be elected.

Resolved 6th. That the secretary tender an invitation to those in the neighboring States and in the Nation, who wish to go to California, to join the company."

The article went on to list several more items, and then began an invitation to non-Cherokee immigrants to travel with them.

"This company will leave the first of April, if the grass will justify a company starting so early, if not, just as soon as possible.

All persons or parts of Companies forming at the following places: Fayetteville and Bentonville, Ark., Sarcoxie, Cowskin Prairie, Springfield, Mo., are cordially invited to join with us.

There is one very great advantage in going with the Cherokee company. The Cherokees are on the most friendly terms with all the Indian tribes of the Prairie- - consequently there will be no danger of attacks from our red brethren."

Willie pondered over the last part of the letter. It was highly unusual for the Cherokees to want to band together with non-Cherokees. However, he had to concede that there was safety in numbers. Upon arriving home that night, he decided he would have to be more forthright with Clara. He had already made his decision, but he did have some worries over the coming birth of their baby. After feeding and bedding down his animals for the night, he knocked the dirt from his worn boots and entered the cabin. Clara was standing by the stove, pots bubbling and steaming with a pleasant aroma. She wore a blue calico "Cherokee tear dress" which did a lot to conceal the rising bump of her expanding belly.

"Dinner will be ready right quick, Willie. Wash up before you come to the table. I almost have everything ready," said Clara.

Willie turned aside to a ewer and wash basin in the corner. The water was so cold it was almost frozen where the basin sat close to the door. He rolled up his shirtsleeves and washed up to his elbows. The bitter cold of the water surprised him, but he knew it would be cozy in the kitchen or next to their fireplace. After toweling his skin dry, he sat down at the head of the small table while she poured out the contents of the pan into a large soup bowl. They ate in strained silence. Each one sat waiting for the other to speak, what was most on their mind. It seemed to be a painful thing, now. Where could he start?

"The fields are still too frozen to do much clearing. I suppose it will have to wait until I get back in a few months time," said Willie.

Clara narrowed her eyes and a look of disgust crossed her face.

"If you think this – fools errand – you are pursuing will only take a few months, you are lying to yourself," said Clara.

Willie took a long breath, trying to gain a measure of time to give a good answer.

"Clara, you are right, of course. I have no idea how long it will take. Not really. I can only say that I will come back as quick as I can. I only want enough gold to get our farm up and going. Perhaps, I could buy us a couple of slaves to help us. Don't you think I want to be here with you, if I could? Of course I do. But this is an opportunity we just can't pass up. All the reports say, that the gold is just lying around on the ground and all you have to do is bend down to pick it up. How hard can that be? It should only take me a little while to gather enough to come home and then everything about our lives will be better. You'll see, it will turn out well for us," said Willie, anguish and hope spilling out of his voice.

Clara was not convinced. She looked down at her ballooning abdomen and then looked sharply up at Willie.

"What am I supposed to do while you are gone? I am pregnant and unable to plow. How will I feed myself? How will I live? And who will help me with the birthing? You have not thought this out well enough. Only for you, but not for me," said Clara, tears running down her round cheeks, but determination in her eyes.

Willie was startled. He had thought about these very questions and also had worked out a solution. He just had not told her. What a terrible oversight.

"Darling, I am so sorry. I have neglected to tell you how I planned this out to help you while I am gone. You see, I asked Martha Samson, the next farm over, to look in and see about you. I have pledged a portion of my take of gold for your upkeep. Both Martha and Daniel will help to take care of the animals I don't take with me and when your time comes, you will move over to their place for the birthing. You see? I have thought of you. I am doing this for both of us. But you must allow me the time to make our fortune," said Willie.

No matter how much Clara cried or complained, Willie felt he was doing the best for the both of them and he continued to pull together the things he would need for the trip. Clara finally stood by, watching with doleful eyes and a feeling of abandonment in her heart.

For Willie, the lure of easy money had him spellbound. Any man, any man at all who was willing to travel to the gold fields of California and scoop up the gold from the ground, was entitled to the riches he received. He would let nothing stand in the way of his dream.

Chapter 4

In Tahlequah, things were proceeding quickly. Every day, new and interested Cherokees were inquiring about the trip and what would be needed. But James Vann, the editor of the Cherokee Advocate Newspaper, was becoming increasingly nervous about the route they would take. A few months earlier Josiah Gregg had published his account of the many times he traveled the southern route to Santa Fe. He had led at least nine expeditions of California or Oregon bound immigrants. In his writing, Mr. Gregg talked of the ease and efficacy of that route and also reported that the grass, which was so important for the animals drawing the wagons, was up almost one month earlier than the trail from Independence, Missouri.

However, he was worried about possible encounters with the southern tribes of the prairies. Living on the edge of the western frontier and because Indian Territory was filled with Native tribes, they would hear first of any attacks happening close to their borders. There had been several reports coming in concerning the southern trail and Vann began to have a glimmer of doubt about the proposed route. He had just received a copy of an article printed in the St. Louis Reveille in February. It read:

Col. Gilpin writes, that a large body of Indians and renegade Mexicans are collecting upon the Canadian (River), for the purpose of general marauding in the spring. There have been several thousand animals and oxen stolen in the trail last summer —The Comanches, Kiowas, Apaches, and Pawnees, are floating about in large parties. A party of Taos and Apaches a few weeks ago killed three teamsters and burned their wagons.

In his office, Vann discussed the problem with his secretary, Miles Bates.

"Miles, I am not certain that we should take Josiah Gregg's route. Look at this report. If this band of renegades accosted us, we could lose everything overnight and I, for one, am not willing for this venture to fail so quickly. What do you think?" said James Vann.

"I see what you mean. But, what other way is there? Josiah's route has been traveled for many years and is well known. It seemed a good road for us. Now, I am not sure," replied Miles.

"The fact that it is well known is what is causing the problem. The renegades know that there will be travelers on that road. We would be walking into a trap, that we were totally aware would happen, if we took that route. I have been thinking that we might consider blazing a new trail. We could all meet at some predetermined spot, get organized there and find a way of slipping past the renegades and warring Indians. Plus, this other article, we wrote, inviting even non-Cherokees to join with us in our company is something I hope will be considered. There are advantages to banding together with the whites and advantages for them as well. Like the article says, we are on friendly terms with the Indians of the prairies. It could save them a lot of trouble and heartache in the long run," said James Vann.

Miles stood a moment and shook his head slowly. He seemed to be worried about the prospect.

"James, I don't mean to disagree, but the most obvious problem in that scheme is the inability of some whites to work peacefully with the Cherokees. You are asking for some real trouble. You can't change men's nature overnight, just because it would make the way safer," said Miles.

James walked over to the window and looked out at the bustling town below. In his mind, it would be the lesser of two evils. Safety on the trail should be paramount to everyone. As far as he was concerned, the whites were people, just like any other people. The fact was the Cherokee were more like whites now than Indians. They could read and write, had schools and churches, they even had their own government. It still looked like the best answer to everyone's problems. Banding together with the white company would save lives. If one of the men in the white company was uncomfortable with it, he could always join a different company.

"No, I can't look at it that way. There is too much at stake including our lives to get squeamish over race. I shall write a letter to the Fayetteville newspaper and ask to be put in contact with the organizer of the white company.

They may not want to go with us, but we shall see what they say," said James Vann, with finality.

*****

In another part of the Cherokee Nation, young Danica Mosley read the news about the many companies of immigrants readying to leave for the gold fields of California. A large majority of them would leave using the Santa Fe Trail, which began in Independence, Missouri. William Becknell had pioneered that route back in 1821, connecting Independence to Santa Fe, New Mexico. It was a well-traveled route and had been used by wagon trains going to Oregon and California. However, the Cherokee Advocate newspaper seemed to say, that the groups forming in Indian Territory would leave using a southern route.

But that was beside the point for Danica. She was a woman alone in the world, since her husband of only three years died last fall, leaving her with a one hundred acre farm. She yearned to go to the gold fields and stake her claim to whatever future she could make. She was sure that some men would take their wives, if they were tough enough, to California. She doubted that a woman with no man would be accepted into one of the companies. Danica despaired over the choices she would have to make to reach a goal that would be unthinkable to most women.

After reading the last news article on the gold strikes in California, she lay the newspaper down, staring off into space. She tried to visualize the steps she would need to take, but she knew the reality would be much worse. Was she strong enough? Did she possess the courage needed? She did not know. Once she embarked on accomplishing her scheme, there would be no turning back.

She walked to the bedroom where a tall-framed mirror stood in its own stand. Given to her for her wedding, it was one of a few things she cherished. She looked long and hard at herself, then, slowly began taking the pins out of her long blackish brown hair. It seemed that everything that made a woman, a woman, was tied to the crown of her hair. Men desired women with long luxurious locks that would shine in the light. Her hair was just as beautiful as she could have wanted. Now hanging down below her waist, straight and strong she ran her fingers through it again and again. Then holding back tears, she found her husband's straight razor and began cutting off chunks of hair close to her scalp, letting the hanks fall slowly to the floor. Anger overcame her as she cut faster and faster, until she was cutting at a furious rate. The dark handfuls of straight hair silently mounding at her feet, but only her own ears could hear her weeping.

The next steps would be to bind herself, so that her bosom did not show. It would be painful at first, but she would get used to it, she thought. A woman cherished her womanly parts, but she would be forced to deny them. She could not, would not, turn aside from her decision as tears fell to the floor.

Then she worked at fitting her husband's clothes to her body. She would make a small man, but she knew people saw only what they wanted to see. She could not grow a beard, so she solved that problem with smudging a thin layer of boot black on her cheeks. Only enough to look like a shadow. Once she had converted herself, she set about putting together the needed supplies, as outlined in the paper.

She would test her disguise first, by going into Tahlequah to buy what supplies she did not already possess. If she could pass that test, she believed she would be at least accepted as a young man and a willing immigrant to the gold fields of California.

Chapter 5

Sasa and Coyote had spent many days helping Jackson prepare for the onslaught of immigrants wishing to buy mules from him. There was already a high demand and Jackson was having a hard time keeping up with the requests for good animals to draw the wagons. Sasa had had little time to spend alone with her husband, Coyote.

Coyote was Sioux and Northern Blackfoot. His tribes lay far to the north. Coyote had been an intelligent child, learning at the foot of the medicine man. Although, he knew as much about fighting, as the next warrior, Coyote did not consider himself to be a warrior. He would rather find ways to make peace and for that his tribe ridiculed him. He had stayed with the Sioux, where his mother also lived, until adulthood, then set off in a southerly direction to find a new life. He had found it with Sasa and her family.

On the other hand, Sasa, although a full blood Cherokee, had set a goal as a teenager to learn all she could about the white world, so that she could help her people. She agreed to be the ward of Jackson Halley, at that time not married yet to Anna, and he promised to give her a white man's education so that she could accomplish her goal. Just a few short years of intense education, by the best tutor's money could buy, and she was presented to Boston society and was warmly accepted, by most. There had been a few unjustly biased against her Indian heritage, but they had long been won over by her charm and grace. Still, Sasa's heart lay in Indian Territory and helping her people. After meeting Coyote and helping him to learn English, they fell in love.

They had been married nearly a year and the bloom of the fine wedding, last summer, had not worn off. She remembered very well the day of her wedding. It had been done in Cherokee fashion and the festivities went on all day. There were many ritual dances among the men of the tribe and the women danced with their shawls swinging in the breeze. A central drum was set up, with many drummers and singers surrounding it. A fire burned close by, which helped to light the dancer's way as night fell.

Sasa had worn a totally white buckskin dress, with long fringes from her shoulders and arms to the ground. Intricate beadwork adorned the yoke of her dress and a beaded belt wrapped around her tiny waist. Her moccasins were a solid mass of beading, which had taken over a year to make by one of the tribe's matrons.

Coyote was like-wise dressed in finery, but of Lakota design. He wore a beaded buckskin shirt and a breach cloth, painted and adorned with beading. His leggings matched his shirt and he had drawn up his long black hair and placed feathers and dangling beads into it. He wore specially beaded cuffs and a beaded belt with long fringe around his waist. Sasa's breath had been taken away at the sight of him.

The wedding feast was something everyone would remember for years to come. But now it was hard for Sasa not to be a little jealous of the time, which Jackson's business was taking so much of. Even in the limited time that she saw him, Sasa knew that something else was bothering Coyote. She had seen it in him the last few days and she was concerned as to what it might be. That night in their little cabin, she decided it was time to find out.

"Coyote, something is on your mind. I know Jackson has been working you hard the last few days, but I get the feeling something else is bothering you. Please, my love, tell me what it is. You know I am happy to listen, to whatever it is," said Sasa.

Coyote looked at her with piercingly serious eyes. He seemed to consider whether or not to tell her, what was in his heart. He was not afraid to talk in English, these days, because he had mastered the language very well and spoke it with barely an accent.

Finally, a slight smile crept over his lips and he took her by the hands, drawing her close to his chest, and wrapping his arms around her tenderly.

"To be honest, yes, there is something that I have been thinking about. I have to confess, I am not sure how you will react to an idea I have had. But, since you have asked me in your bold way, I will have to tell you," said Coyote.

Sasa took a breath and squeezed him tightly, then letting herself be held at arms-length, Coyote spoke to her.

"I suppose I have caught "gold fever"; everyone else has. Jackson says, that is what the newspapers are calling it now. I think, I want to go with the Cherokee on their trip to the gold fields. One thing though has been bothering me. I don't want to go without you and I was not sure if you would want to go as well. It is likely to be a hard trip and almost anything could happen. I would not have you harmed. At the same time, I believe we may pass over my people's traditional lands and I think I might be needed to smooth the way," said Coyote.

Sasa slowly lowered herself down into a chair. This was the last thing she would have thought of bothering him. But, now that she thought of it, it was a natural thing for Coyote to want to have another adventure. Why not? However, were any of the other men taking their wives? She had not read anything about that, so she would have to make inquiries. She herself had not had any burning desire to go find gold. She was happy with her life as it was. But, she wanted Coyote to be happy too.

"If we were to go, we would have to take Wheezer and of course Yellow Eyes?" said Sasa, questioningly.

"Yes I realize that, but I can make sure Yellow Eyes stayed with me and Wheezer always stays with you anyway. Most of the Cherokee are familiar with Yellow Eyes, even though he is a wild coyote. They've gotten used to him being with me. And I can assure the white men he will cause no trouble," said Coyote.

"Dearest, let me first find out if any other women are going with their husbands, and then we can decide what to do. I will write to James Vann, at the Advocate. He is an old friend and also a Cherokee. I am sure he will know. If there are going to be other Cherokee women on the trip, then I have no objections to going with you, with one condition. That we don't stay in California. We must eventually come home, to my family, no matter what happens, whether, we find gold or not. Is that something you can live with?" said Sasa.

Coyote smiled broadly, kissing her on the forehead and then her hand. He was very happy with her answer, and excited at the prospect of this unusual trip.

*****

Stan had awakened, in a dusty room, with only a cot and a small table beside him. On the table was a glass of water and a small lamp. He could hear the wind whipping around the lone building outside and it made him shiver. Blood soaked his shirt and a rough bandage was tied around his chest. He felt groggy, but the pain in his chest let him know that he was alive. He remembered little of the man who had taken him to safety. He had no idea where he was. Nor who was caring for him now.

He thought of all the planning and preparing he had done for his trip and how fleeting it all was. He despaired of his injuries, not knowing how bad they might be. He gazed at the sunlight streaming through the only window, the dust motes swirling around and around. He thought, that is what I am, just a bit of dust, blown about. Now his family would have to suffer.

After some time the door to the room opened and a tall man dressed in leather entered. He looked at Stan with inquiring eyes.

"Hello, my name is Albertson, James Albertson. I am the doctor hereabouts. I see you have had a nasty encounter with someone with a gun. Can you tell me who did this to you and maybe a little about why?" said Dr. Albertson, as he stood close to the bed.

Stan thought for a few moments. What did he remember? What good would it do him now, even if he knew who his attacker was? He gathered his breath to speak.

"My name is Stan Grant. I live a little ways from Fayetteville and I'm a guessin', that the man that found me, must have brought me here, since, there ain't no doctor in our little village. The best I can remember, I was on my way in my wagon to meet up with others who were formin' a company to go for California and search for gold. I had everythin' I needed for the trip. But someone jumped me on the road, shot me and left me for dead. How bad am I, Doc?" said Stan.

The doctor had a slight smile on his lips and seemed to enjoy the question.

"Well, that's the funny thing. You were shot in the chest, that is true, but as far as I can tell, the bullet did not hit anything vital, not a bone or your lungs. So what you have here is a bad flesh wound. I daresay, you could be up and around in a week or two," answered Dr. Albertson.

Stan thought furiously. He might still be able to join up with a company. But, he had no supplies. He wanted more than anything to catch up to the man who stole his wagon. He would have to ask around in Fayetteville, to see if there was room for a man alone with nothing or no one to speak for him. He had nothing to lose and all that he could do was try.

Chapter 6

The man drove the stolen wagon on and on. For fear of being caught, he decided not to go to Fayetteville to meet up with the company forming there. He would try his luck at finding a place in any company forming in Fort Smith, thereby bypassing, problems with the law in case someone had found the body. He was breathless at what he had done. He hadn't known he had it in him, to kill, but kill he did. He pulled his rough hat down around his ears, to fight the bitter cold and the blustery wind as he drove.

It would all be worth it in the end, he thought. He would make his fortune at the gold fields, and then could go anywhere he pleased. He chuckled at the prospect. He was going to be rich and would not let anything stop him, least of all, a stupid farmer who seemed to have everything.

So on down the road he went, dreaming of his triumph and success. Gloating at how easy it had been to take the wagon and dispose of the driver. He was on his way, finally.

* * * * *

By March, 1849, Captain Evans' company and the company of the Cherokees had exchanged letters concerning the joining of the two parties together for safety sake. It seemed agreeable and Evans could not foresee any problems coming from the combined companies. The official name would now be the Evans/Cherokee Company.

However, there were somewhat heated discussions about the road they would take. Evans was especially adamant, that they not take the southern route. His friend, David, was not so sure.

"But you won't really know where you're going. You could come upon some Indian encampment and then where will you be?" said David.

"Look, we already know that there are Indian raiders poised on the southern route, to rob and kill us. I have no intention of walking into the arms of thieves, especially when I know they are there. Can our making a new road across the prairies, be more dangerous than that?" asked Evans.

"I only hope you know what you are doing Evans. This has never been done before," said David.

"No? Well, it has, but only by the many mountain men headed for the mountains. They made their own trail. It was the Cherokee's idea to blaze a new trail and I agree. So there's the end to it," said Evans, with finality.

So far the Evans Company had acquired immigrants from Evansville, Middle Fork of White River, several from Washington County, Benton County, Huntsville in Madison County, and Fayetteville in Arkansas. Also, some arrived from as far north as Springfield, Missouri.

The Cherokee company included at least three married couples, and five unnamed slaves, besides the large group of Cherokee men assembling for the trip. All the travelers were to meet at Lewis Ross' establishment, at the Grant Saline, near the old salt works. Parties had been arriving for days, knowing that the Evan/Cherokee Company was to leave by April 24th, if the grass was up high enough for the grazing of the animals.

When the majority of the combined travelers had arrived at Lewis Ross', they held a meeting to establish elected officers. Each man had to sign a contract that stipulated that he would abide by the decisions of the elected officers. This contract is one thing that would help to hold them together, if the going got tough. The Cherokees, even though they would abide by the stipulated rules, separated themselves by forming a separate division called, Oo-Cha-Loo-Ta. Some of the Cherokees in the group were: Martin Matthew Schrimpsher, Walt J. B Smith, Oliver Wack Lipe (a white married to Cherokee Catherine Gunter), James S. Vann, R. L. Coleman, Daniel M. Gunter, J. C. McMaster, brothers George W. and Richard N. Keys, Josiah N. Rattlingourd, N. R. N. Harlin, Joseph H. Sturdevant, Robert Williams, William P. McKey, and white schoolteacher Sam Potter and others.

At least, forty wagons formed the combined company and Lewis Evans was again elected Company Captain. There were also men elected to other positions of responsibility. Second or 1st Lieutenant in command was Thomas Lyons, 2nd Lieutenant was Peter Mankins, 1st Sargent Joseph Waits, 2nd Sargent George North, 3rd Sargent Squire Marrs. There were four divisions and each had a Division Wagon Master. Each division was made up of ten wagons. The Cherokees were one of the divisions. James S.

Vann, the former Editor of the Cherokee Advocate Newspaper was elected Secretary for the whole company. Upon his leaving the Cherokee Advocate printed this article:

James S. Vann, the former Editor of this paper took his leave for the Gold regions in California. We understand that on the 24th or 25th the company that rendezvoused at Grand River. Set out for the far west with about forty wagons in company and the rise of more than 100 persons....

Our fellow citizens and friends have been dropping off for California for some eight or ten days - - the last of them from about this section started on last Monday (April 23) casting long and wistful looks upon the land of their homes and nativity.

They all have the prayers and good wishes of their friends and relations for their peace and prosperity, hoping that a kind and beneficent Deity will preserve them from the pestilence that walketh in darkness.

Sasa, Coyote and Wheezer arrived after the election of officers. They found the camp crowded with excited and jubilant men and a few women. Jackson had supplied their wagon and supplies and they were as ready for the adventure as any of the others. On the night before they left the Grand Saline, Coyote was approach by a lone man who held his left arm close to his body. Wheezer barked a couple of times then stopped, cocked his head and waited. The man looked a little shy about approaching them, but Sasa's warm smile brought him closer.

"I hope you don't mind me interruptin', my name is Stan Grant. I got here by beggin' a ride from one of the other wagons, and I walked part of the way too", said Stan.

Stan then proceeded to tell his story to them. This had been the sixth time he had approached a traveler in this group. He had been turned down all five times. Now he was hoping that these Indians and their dog would take pity on him in exchange for work. But, when he saw Yellow Eyes, he was taken aback at the sight of a wild coyote so close to humans.

"Sir, if you would not mind giving my husband and I a moment to talk, we will let you know our answer shortly," said Sasa.

Sasa and Coyote walked a little way into the darkness, while Wheezer and Yellow Eyes stayed to watch over him. Coyote could sense the humanity in Sasa and knew what she would have to say.

"Coyote, it is certainly terrible that this man almost died trying to make it to this wagon train. I know, he has nothing to give other than work, but he says he is a good hunter. And besides, you have been asked to help scout for the group. That will take you away from me for many hours of the day. It would be nice to have him here to talk to and in case we are attacked," said Sasa.

But Coyote had already come to the same conclusion. He had worried about Sasa being alone to drive the wagon by herself, while he scouted for any trouble up ahead. So he nodded his head in agreement and they went back to where Stan stood to give him the news.

Stan breathed a sign of relief. This was the last chance he had of going with this group. He had to go now. If he had not been able to get someone to except this barter, he would have had to return home and he could not bare the thought of failure, before he had even gotten started. However, he also had a second mission. He planned on finding the stolen wagon if it was traveling in this group. He would find it and take it back. And when he discovered the thief, he would dispense his own form of justice.

The next morning the four divisions of the train organized into a long line of wagons and the trip began. There were one hundred twenty nine people, with 40 wagons, three hundred and four oxen, thirty-one cows, forty-one mules and sixty-five horses. All were setting out on a journey with no road. They would blaze the road as they progressed.

Chapter 7

The first few days were tiresome and grueling. It had rained on the prairie which turned the ground into muddy mire. The first day, the wagons only made fifteen miles. Much time was spent pulling or digging wagons out of mud holes. They camped at Prior's Creek and all of the company was glad to rest for the night. Years later, the town of Pryor, Oklahoma would be established close to this site.

Again, the second day was just as difficult. They only made five miles that day and stopped at a place they named Coral. It was here, during the night, they lost several of their oxen, apparently they decided, they liked it better at the previous camp. The company sent out riders to go back and drive them to the wagon train. It took them until the next night to catch up to the train, dirty and exhausted. They would have to find a better way of picketing the oxen.

The third day brought them to the divide where Prior Creek and the Verdigris River converge. The cold rain and freezing drizzle had stopped, giving the ground a chance to dry out. There were many chores to attend to each night, before the company could settle down to rest. Alexander Crawford, the First Division Wagon Master, spent his free time writing in a journal about the happenings of each day and logging the distance traveled as best he could.

Sasa noticed that, on the occasions when Coyote wasn't scouting, Coyote and Stan seemed to get along well. Wheezer spent his days chasing rabbits or sniffing down gopher holes, then catching up to Sasa's wagon. When he tired of his play, he would jump up into the wagon and fall asleep on the tarps covering the supplies in the back. Yellow Eyes stayed at Coyote's side, while he scouted ahead on his mule.

The Company seemed in good spirits. Even Danica Mosely who now called herself, Dan, felt lighthearted. She kept to herself, never spoke up and knew better than to complain. After a week on the trip, Dan overheard what could have bloomed into a very heated argument.

Henley Hughes was from Washington County, Arkansas. He had a deep and abiding hatred of all Indians. He was not happy with the decision to combine the Cherokee company with the white one. He saw no good reason to trust the Cherokees.

"Someone took my best draw knife. You parked your wagon behind mine last night and you are the most likely to have taken it. Give it back. Now!" demanded Henley.

Albert Langley also had agreed to come with the Cherokee company, before the two companies combined. But, he did not hold any hatred for any of his fellow man. In fact, he did everything he could to adapt to white ways, just as his tribe had been doing for decades.

"Sir, I assure you, I do not have your draw knife. I've never been inside your wagon. I have my own draw knife; in fact I have more than one. You are welcome to come and see what I have, but none of them is yours," said Albert.

"I doubt you would keep it with your own things. Sneaky Injuns, that's what you people are. I knew this would not work, from the very start. You shouldn't even be here with us. Go and make your own train," said Henley.

The argument went on like this for several minutes, until another of the white men approached them.

"Henley, he didn't take anythin' and you been makin' a fool of yourself. Don't you remember? You lent me your draw knife yesterday, so's I could scrape down one of my spare spokes in case I needs it," said the man.

Henley looked around at the onlookers who had begun to gather to watch the argument. Realizing his mistake, but not wanting to lose face in front of some dirty Indian, Henley growled and stepped into his wagon without another word.

Some of the onlookers had nodded their heads when Henley had voiced his distrust of the Cherokees and this did not bode well for the trip to come.

Coyote had also gathered there to watch the argument. It gave him chills to think the train was not a unified unit. He had never anticipated prejudice, because he had assumed that all the white men had agreed to join with the Cherokees. Now he knew that he and Sasa would need to be on their guard.

That night, while most everyone slept, Wheezer and Yellow Eyes patrolled the camp, making sure all was well for the people. The fires had burned down some and the embers only produced a dim light. As they came around one of the wagons, Wheezer noticed someone was up and moving around inside. Someone was moving stealthily, as if trying to keep quiet. Wheezer and Yellow Eyes stopped in their tracks and waited. Suddenly, they heard two hard thumps, then, all went quiet. Wheezer gave a low growl, but when nothing else was heard, they lost interest and continued on their rounds, until finally they snuggled up to Sasa, asleep in the wagon, alongside Coyote.

The next morning, everyone was up and preparing their breakfast. Usually, a meal made up of flapjacks or biscuits with bacon gravy. The weather would be fair that day; the morning was fresh and clean. After breakfast, the men began to hitch up their animals to the wagons. All the wagons were almost ready, except for one. Coyote noticed that he had not seen Albert Langley that morning. His wagon was two wagons up from Langley's and it seemed that no one was gathering any animals and hitching up the team.

Coyote signaled to Wheezer and Yellow Eyes to come with him as he went towards Albert's wagon, calling his name a few times. When no one answered, Coyote began to look around the wagon and finally stepped up inside the back. There is where he found Albert. He lay in a pool of his own blood, in the walkway in the center of his wagon. His head was beaten in savagely. Nothing could have prepared Coyote for the sight. But, Coyote kept looking around, taking note of how the body lay and everything around it. Then, Wheezer began barking until finally Sasa appeared at the back of Albert's wagon.

"What is wrong with Wheezer? What's going on? Where is Albert anyway?" asked Sasa.

Coyote did not answer right away. He continued looking for anything that could tell him what had happened. As he stepped toward the exit, his foot stepped on something hard and metallic. It made a slight noise. He picked it up and looked at it; holding it up, he could see it was a broken silver chain with a dangling cross. He had no idea if it belonged to Albert or his killer. He slipped it into the medicine bag that hung around his neck. Coyote came out, stepping down from the wagon, so that he could find Captain Evans.

"Don't go in, Sasa. Albert is dead. Someone bashed his head in and it looks like it happened sometime last night. The blood is dry in places. It had to have happened last night some time. But, I have no clue as to who did this. I guess, Albert did not cry out or we would have heard him. I'm not sure why anyone would kill him. He was a pretty likable Cherokee. He did have an argument with Henley Hughes yesterday. We all saw that, but that does not mean he did this. I have to go and get Captain Evans. I will be back," said Coyote. Then he strode away.

While Sasa stood there waiting for Coyote to return with Captain Evans, she saw in the distance, to the east, a rider leading a horse. As the figures got closer, she recognized Peter Diggins. She was astonished, that she had not remembered, that Peter was Albert's traveling partner and therefore, should have been in the wagon too. Where had he been last night? Why was he not in the wagon with Albert sleeping?

Peter pulled his horse up to the wagon and dismounted.

"Hello Sasa. Why doesn't Albert have the wagon hitched up to the oxen? They are almost ready to start," said Peter.

"*Osiyo* (Hello in Cherokee) Peter, I am so sorry to have to tell you this, but last night Albert was killed, in fact murdered. His body is still in the wagon and Coyote has gone for Captain Evans. Where were you last night? Why weren't you here?" asked Sasa.

Peter was aghast. How could his partner, to the gold fields, be dead? When Peter calmed down a mite, he answered.

"Our mare ran off yesterday after it got loose from the wagon. We had it tethered to the back of the wagon, while we rode up front. No one noticed until we camped, so I had to go after her. It took me all night to find her and bring her back. Who would do this to Albert? He wouldn't hurt a fly!" said Peter.

Sasa paused briefly and heaved a sigh.

"We don't know much now, we only just found him. I expect this may delay today's travel. When Captain Evans gets here, I imagine he will see if there were any witnesses. That is all I know. Do not go inside the wagon, yet, until Captain Evans takes a look. Coyote is the one who discovered him and I believe he looked around some, but I don't think there is anything in there that we can draw any conclusions from, other than he died some time last night," said Sasa.

Peter waited obediently by the wagon, until Captain Evans arrived with Coyote and three of the division Wagon Masters. Captain Evans went into the wagon alone and was inside for a few minutes. When he emerged the pallor of his skin had whitened and his expression was of deep dismay.

"For the life of me, I can't understand why anyone would do this. It is obvious that it has to be someone on the wagon train, because we haven't seen any strangers approach us, since we left the Grand Saline. Therefore, all we can do is give the man a decent burial and go on. Maybe along the way, we will discover something that will help us to understand, what happened here. Make no mistake gentlemen, those elected men, who you all placed in their positions, will now be more vigilant about the security of the train. We will all need to cooperate with whatever they deem necessary to keep all our people safe," said Captain Evans.

Alexander Crawford stepped forward and asked, "Has anyone come forward as a witness to anything unusual happening last night? Someone must have heard something."

Just at that moment, Wheezer, standing by Sasa, began to bark and turn in circles. But, the men thought he just wanted to bark at something that moved in the grass and they paid no mind. All except Sasa, who knew that Wheezer was trying to communicate, something important.

After the crowd dispersed, Sasa and Wheezer went back to their wagon. She stopped and bent down to talk with him.

"What's going on boy? Did you see something last night?" asked Sasa.

Again Wheezer barked and turned in circles.

"Alright, Wheezer, it's alright. I know you can't tell me what you saw, but I want you to keep watch over the people at night. You and Yellow Eyes are good at that. Come wake me up if you see or hear anything. Understand Wheezer? Wake me up if anything happens at night," said Sasa.

Most people would think she was foolish, to speak to a dog in such a way, but Wheezer had shown, many times, his ability to understand and obey. Wheezer and Yellow Eyes seemed to have a language, unto themselves, so she trusted Wheezer to tell his friend.

Chapter 8

After a brief religious ceremony for Albert, the wagon train got underway again and that day they completed only five miles.

Captain Evans wanted to assemble the entire train together, but since he had no witnesses and nothing to identify who had committed the murder, decided it would be a fruitless exercise. But, he would not forget what happened.

The next day was Saturday, which was a trying day for all. Alexander Crawford wrote in his diary:

"we got to the Verdigris River last night, and it took us all this day till late this evening to dig down the banks and cross over. Ten miles today."

They traveled on, day after day. The weather was getting milder and warmer, by increments. The voyage seemed agonizingly slow, but they all knew, each day brought them one step closer to their goal.

Then, the prairie changed from rolling hills to flatter land. Crawford wrote:

"It will be two weeks Tuesday since we left home and we have not eaten but one ham and two thirds of the middling of our bacon....

There has not been any game killed on our route yet except some turkeys. We are in a world of prairie; you may see here as far as your eyes will let you look. We have encamped in a beautiful part of the prairie.

...the prairies are very good and dry...Our sleeping is first rate, our bed is plenty soft.

Then one day, Coyote spotted a group of Indians. They were too far away from the wagons, to be seen by them, but Coyote was anxious that all should go well with this meeting. It would set the tone for the rest of the trip. Thankfully they turned out to be Osage. Because of his friendship with the Osage and the fact that he spoke their language, there was no trouble. But Crawford wrote:

The Osages tell us that we will have to fight the Pawnees and Comanches before we get through the mountains. But I think it is uncertain; we may have to fight them, but I hardly think so....

The Osage Indians are coming to our camp every night, they are quite filthy, but very civil. They made a big dance last night for the amusement of our company. I know you would laugh to see them dance and hear them sing. I think they could have been heard singing last night three miles, but I could not note the tune.

Each night the Osage held a dance. Many of the Cherokees joined them. They made a circle in the middle of camp and set up a large drum at the center. No less than five Osage drummed and sang while the others danced. Coyote and Sasa both danced and it was a good time had by all. Only Wheezer was prevented from entering the circle. Animals were not allowed in the dance circle, because their dancing had religious meaning to them. Sasa used the opportunity to change into her deerskin dress, for the occasion. Coyote wore his traditional Lakota clothes.

The days flowed, one into another, and all the men and women seemed to be cooperating together. But, with one hundred twenty-eight people and all the animals it was hard to get to meet everyone. There were still travelers on the train that were unknown to Sasa, Coyote and Stan.

Stan had not taken the time to meet everyone. His injury was healing, but he only moved around when it was absolutely necessary. Then one day, Sasa sent him to take a message to Captain Evans. Evans wagon was at the front of the train and therefore at the other side of the large circle of wagons. Instead of walking across the great expanse where the cook fires had been lit, he took his time and went around the circumference of the circle. With a sudden start, he realized he was walking by a wagon that he recognized as his own. At first he was undecided about what to do. The person claiming his wagon was not there at the moment. If he raised an alarm now, who would believe him? The person, who stole his wagon, could just say he was lying. He backed away from the wagon and after delivering the message, went back to Sasa. Coyote was just coming back from his daily scouting. When Sasa and Coyote were together, Stan asked for a private conversation, to take place inside the wagon. Sensing something serious had happened, Sasa and Coyote agreed.

Sitting on boxes of supplies and bags of flour they listened, while Stan explained what he had seen.

"I don't really know what to do about it. I have no proof, except for one thing," said Stan.

"And what is that one thing?" asked Sasa.

"I loaded all of my own tools into that there wagon and most of them have my initials carved into the wood handles. But, I got no way of forcing the man to let me look inside," said Stan.

"Do you know the man, Stan?" asked Coyote.

"Well, I didn't stick around to see who was driving it. I spose, I shoulda done that, but findin' that wagon about knocked the stuffin' outa me," said Stan, sincerely.

"Then I think we should wait, bide our time and make sure who it is claiming that wagon. I suppose, there is no way to identify the man who left you for dead back in Arkansas?" said Sasa.

"No. He was disguised real good, and after I got shot, I had to play dead so's he didn't finish me off. I know it don't help me none neither," said Stan.

"Well, let's not get ahead of ourselves, for the time being. We have plenty of time before we have to do anything about it. I will do a little asking around and see if I can find out who he is. You just help me like you have been. Don't let on that you know anything. For all you know, he may have already spotted you and we don't want you put into any danger, especially, after the murder of Albert the other night. There might be a connection. It is best we see how things work out first," said Sasa.

Stan agreed to the plan and stepped down from the wagon. Wheezer, who had waited patiently for him to come out, greeted him. Since Stan had been doing part of the driving of the wagon every day, Wheezer believed

Stan was now part of his pack. Yellow Eyes, on the other hand, stuck close to Coyote and remained distrustful of most other humans.

Chapter 9

Dan Mosely had been silently watching the movements of the various wagon owners from day to day. She had tried to be pleasant, but not necessarily friendly with her neighbors. By watching them, she learned a lot about how to function on the trail. She had especially learned from her Cherokee brothers and the young woman Sasa. She had never seen a woman of the Cherokee, who seemed to know just what to do, and her dog was the smartest she had ever encountered. It was a joy to watch him play with Sasa and Coyote.

But, there was one of her neighbors that puzzled her greatly. He was a lone man in a wagon. He almost never spoke to anyone and he kept his large hat pulled down over his eyes. She would not have noticed him, except that she had done the same when she first joined the train, in order to conceal her identity. This fact made her suspicious of the man. He seemed to only say what was absolutely necessary and then only short sentences or just one word. The other travelers had taken note of his standoffishness and steered clear of him. However, something was telling Dan that this man could be dangerous and since she had no one to watch her back, she decided to keep a sharp eye on his movements.

At the end of one bright sun drenched day, while they were still on the prairie, Dan noticed that the man had been skulking around the wagons. The man was looking at one particular person on the train and it appeared to be either Sasa or Stan, the helper they had taken on. The sun was beginning to sink and it would be time to start the fires for cooking, but her curiosity was getting the better of her. At a leisurely pace, she followed well behind him, being careful to be looking the other way if he turned around. He stopped about fifty feet from Sasa and Coyote's wagon. Stan appeared from the back of the wagon carrying the cook pan and utensils from dinner. The man stood perfectly still and watched intently, then, all of a sudden he turned and quickly walked back to his own wagon, passing Dan as he went.

Now Dan was sure that the man was watching Stan. But, the reason was unknown to her. Watching him skulk around, made the hair stand up on the back of her neck. He was up to something, but she just could not figure out it was. At the same time, everyone was a little anxious about the death of Albert. There was no way to figure out who had done such a terrible thing and the only thing left to do, was to keep going.

* * * * *

It had been a beautiful, mild, but sunny day and Sasa was glad to stop and watch the sun go down. Coyote had already come back in from his scouting and Stan was starting the cook fire, not too far from the wagon. There was no wood to speak of, no trees or even bushes to glean firewood from. So now, they had to use, the dried excrement, from the huge herds of buffalo. The men called them 'Buffalo Chips' and they provided a good and hot fire. Stan and Sasa had gone out from camp, several times over the last few days, to gather a quantity of chips and store them in the back of the wagon. The sun had baked them dry and they no longer smelt bad at all. Sometimes, there were so many chips available around the camp that they did not have to go searching for them.

That day, they had seen their first buffalo herd, if you could call a mass of buffalo as far as the eye could see, a herd. The wagon master was careful to not spook the animals, in case of a stampede. The wagons had to come to a halt at mid-day and had to wait for the herd to pass. It took at least three hours, so that day they kept traveling until the sun began to settle. They still made fifteen miles, which was close to normal for a day's travel.

While Stan tended the fire, Sasa sat down in the back of the wagon. Coyote dismounted from his horse, tied it to the back of the wagon and joined her.

"What a day today was. That herd of buffalo was amazing. I don't think I will ever see anything as magnificent as that again," said Sasa.

"Oh, there are more things here on the prairie, than you might imagine. Here, you can see further, than you ever will anywhere else. There is a certain time of year when my tribe burns the old grass. It is usually in the early spring, like now," said Coyote.

"What? Doesn't that become a wildfire? I should think it would endanger your people," said Sasa.

"No, the Medicine Man decides when the time is right and where to start the burn. He also knows the direction of the wind and how far the burn will go. That is one of the most important jobs he has. It is the burning of the grass that brings forth the greenest grasses, and that in turn attracts the herds of buffalo to our area. Without burning the grass, we might starve. Up north, where I am from, it probably still has snow on the ground, so it is not time for the burning," said Coyote.

"Do people get caught in the wildfire as it burns?" asked Sasa.

"Sometimes travelers do, but there are ways to avoid it and most tribes of the prairie know how. It is not very often we hear of a death from the burning of the grass," said Coyote.

Sasa looked at her husband with loving eyes. There was so much he could teach her. Some of the wisdom from his tribe was beneficial advice for Indian Territory. Part of the prairie extended down into the territory to the west of Cherokee lands. The Cherokee were still learning about their new land and the best way to survive in a place that was much drier than where they came from in the east.

"Coyote, I love you so much. I am proud and glad to be your wife. I hope we will always be together," said Sasa.

Coyote looked startled. He was not used to hearing endearing remarks from Sasa.

"You already know that I love you too. We are one, together, and we will stay together as long as you and I live," said Coyote.

Stan approached them with a worried look.

"I wanted to tell you, that I noticed that man we saw with my wagon was watchin' us. Well I ain't sure it was us.

It coulda just abeen me he was awatchin'. Even though I saw him plain as day, I still couldn't make out his face. He had his hat pulled way down. So, I think, he must be a knowin', that the owner of that wagon, is here on the train. I'm kinda concerned about it, cause what happened to Albert. I hope somethin' like that won't happen to me," said Stan.

"Now that we know about him, we will make sure that won't happen. I am not sure what exactly will happen, but we know how to defend ourselves," said Sasa.

"I am pretty sure he's white. So we better be careful what we say and who we sayin' it to, if'n, you know what I mean," said Stan.

Yes, Sasa knew exactly what Stan meant. There had been more arguments between the white parts of the train and the Cherokees. Every day there seemed to be another clash between the two races and there was still a long, long way to go. She hoped that it would not fall apart when the going got tough and they needed each other to make it safely to California.

Chapter 10

James Vann and Captain Evans found a quiet place to talk, before the sun completely set. They had been conferring daily on the best route to take. Captain Evans valued James' opinion because the Cherokee were on such good terms with the plains tribes and they seemed to know instinctively, how to blaze this new trail to get to Santa Fe. So far, it had been a relatively easy trip. The Indians they encountered were amiable and in many cases hospitable. But, that might change as they went further north and west.

"That last group of Osage was sure eager to entertain us. I am hoping, that our future relations with the indigenous resident Indians will go as well. We are coming close to the Walnut River. The Osage say there is a crossing, well worn and easy to follow that they have used for many years. Do you suppose we should trust their advice?" said Captain Evans.

"Oh yes, I do. The chief said it was the only good crossing for many miles and that the trail to it is plain as a real road. I don't think they want us here any longer than we have to be, so they are helping us along. We should see the beginnings of that trail by tomorrow mid-day at the latest," said James Vann.

"I'm wondering when we are going to get out of this tall grass with no trees? Sure, we can see as far as a crow can fly, but that is all we see is grass, except for that huge herd of buffalo. But I don't suppose you know the way, any better than I do. Let's hope the rest of our trip goes as well as it has so far.

"I am hoping we won't have any more tense nerves. I've noticed the men seem to be forming groups; Whites vs the Cherokees. Even the group of whites is forming smaller groups, depending on where they originated from. Like all those from Fayetteville and those from Fort Smith. Or even what county they come from. I don't like all this division. If they start to go at each other, we could be in for some unpleasantness. I am going to count on you to help keep a lid on that sort of thing from the Cherokees and I will, for the white factions. It's best to nip this in the bud, before real harm starts," said Captain Evans.

"I've been noticing it myself, Captain. I am hoping that the murder of Albert was not part of that. It would cause a riot on both sides if that murder turned out to be related to skin color. I will do my best if for no other reason than self-preservation. I want to get to California in one piece," said James.

They talked a little while longer before retiring to their own campfires and vittles. The routine of cooking the morning and evening meals was becoming easier as the men learned to use the supplies in the best ways. Cooking enough biscuits at night to have them for breakfast, as well, meant that they would only have to make them once a day. But things like cooked oatmeal and meat did not keep well, so it was better to cook only what one could eat at that meal.

The next day, they came across the Osage trail the chief told them about and they did find the crossing of the Walnut, much easier than they had hoped. The gravel bottom of the crossing was smooth and the banks had been cut down for easy approach and exit from the river. The entire company was happy, that the boasting of the Osage about their trail, proved to be true. The crossed the Walnut with no loss of animals or wagons.

*****

A few days passed in relative calm, save for the relentless swaying of the wagons and the dust kicked up by the turning of the wheels. It was now the first week in May and the weather was holding for them. The route they traveled kept them close to water, the majority of the time, so they did not miss the rain, which would have made the ground a muddy mess.

Sasa, although strong and resilient, was beginning to tire of the featureless landscape and the rolling hills. However, one night she was awakened quite abruptly by Wheezer pushing his nose into her cheek.

"What is it Wheezer? Everyone is asleep, I don't hear anything," said Sasa.

But Wheezer was insistent that she wake up and follow him. Sasa, knowing how perceptive Wheezer could be, obliged him. Dressing quickly, she slipped down from the wagon and proceeded to follow where Wheezer led. They quietly passed several wagons, when Wheezer veered towards the outside perimeter and once there, he began to bark. It was hard for Sasa to see in the dark, but she soon found, that some of the animals that had been corralled inside the circle of wagons, were now roaming freely. Some were quite a way from camp; the moonlight played off of their backs, and revealed where they stood on the far away hills.

Right away, Sasa raised the alarm. Many in the wagons came out sleepy-eyed and groggy, but soon found a reason to wake up fully. Several found their horses and rode out to bring the livestock back to camp. Wheezer helped happily; biting at the heels of the Oxen, hurrying them along. It took a couple of hours, but all the stock was soon recovered.

Coyote and Stan were two of the men on the horses. When they returned to camp, Coyote jumped down from his horse and addressed Captain Evans, who had come to see what the stir was about.

"Sir, I believe if you put hobbles on the Oxen, they would not stray so far, or be so hard to catch," said Coyote.

"Hobbles you say? Not sure why I did not think of that in the beginning. I know how well that works. Hobble an animal and they can graze but not run. I will give the order in the morning, that all livestock is to be hobbled overnight. Now let's get back to bed. We have another long day ahead of us, tomorrow," said Captain Evans.

Sasa, Coyote, Stan and Wheezer walked slowly back towards their wagon. They walked silently, but Sasa held Coyote's hand in the darkness. As they passed one of the wagons, Sasa was startled by and odd noise and something landing in front of them and stuck in the ground at Stan's feet. She stopped to bend down and examine what it was. Picking it up, she was astonished to be holding a very lethal looking knife. Stan grabbed the knife out of her hand and examined it closely.

"This is my own knife. It must have been taken from my wagon. I have a feeling, this is a warning. What do you think, Coyote?" said Stan.

Coyote looked around, but there was no one still up to ask. He would check with the wagon drivers in the morning, to see if anyone saw anything. But Stan was convinced, that it had been the man who now held Stan's wagon as his own. After arriving at their wagon, they sat quietly talking about the knife.

"Stan, how do you know that this is your knife?" asked Coyote.

"Because I carved my initials into the handle, like I did with all of my tools. If that man threw the knife, then he knows now, that we know about his stealin'. I am sure it is a message to stay away from him," said Stan.

"Yes, but why attack you now? I don't understand why he would do something so rash. If I were him, I would lay low and keep to myself," said Sasa.

"Somethin' musta spooked him," said Stan.

"Let's get back to sleep before morning comes, we have a long day ahead of us tomorrow," said Coyote.

As they sat and talked, Yellow Eyes and Wheezer crouched under the wagon, keeping and eye on everything.

*****

In the stolen wagon, the man was beside himself with worry. Why had he panicked? Now those Indians and Stan knew it was him that threw the knife. The subterfuge was beginning to get to his nerves. He had never done anything remotely like this. It was not so hard to waylay Stan, in fact it was fun. He should have made sure he had killed him, instead of walking away from the body. Now, here Stan was, on the same wagon train as him and what could he do about it, nothing. That was why he thought he had needed to send a warning, but now he felt it was a fool thing to do. Up until then, the wagon had been no one's concern. There was no proof that Stan owned it. But, he had just sent them proof, because Stan was sure to recognize that knife.

They had better stay away from him, or he would have to do something drastic. He did not want to draw attention to himself, but if he had to kill Stan all over again, he would. He would let nothing get in the way of his getting to the gold fields and certain riches. Not Stan and not those two Indians he's riding with, either. It was his God given right to be one of the first to get to the gold in California. He would succeed or no one else would.

Chapter 11

Back home in Tahlequah and in Fort Smith, there had been no word from the wagon train. Many felt that they were all dead. The newspapers ran speculative articles about what could have happened to them, but since the wagon train was making their own road, there was no way for letters to get back home. Many were unaware of the isolated nature of this first leg of the trip. One newspaper wrote:

"The Osages and Comanche's are going to togeth-er to intercept, attack, and rob the Fayetteville mining company that lately rendezvous'd at the Grand Saline, and are now on their way to California.... "

Of course it was pure speculation and rumor. Another newspaper wrote:

"We have no very late news from the parties that left here for California. Rumor states that the small company that left from Ft. Gibson has been killed off by the prairie Indians but we do not believe the report."

A few days later, the newspaper reported:

"We have had no…information…from the Fayetteville Mining Company; only that a part of their oxen, some sixteen or eighteen head, have returned to Verdigris River, in the neighborhood of Mr. Elijah Hicks…. Some of our people express uneasiness concerning the company, from the belief that they would not have lost so many cattle, without some difficulty with the prairie Indians. Some again, suppose that they may have been searching for gold on the route, or may have found some, and through their eagerness to obtain the precious stuff, have neglect-ed their cattle. Cherokee Advocate"

The travelers had no idea that so many wild rumors were being bandied about, while they were gone. However, their first opportunity to send letters might be very soon. Once they reached the Santa Fe Trail, there might be ways to get letters to friends and relatives back home. Even when they reached the Santa Fe Trail, they would still be isolated.

*****

Willie Catcher had plodded along on the trail, with all the other wagons, never complaining to anyone about the loneliness of the trip. He missed his Clara profoundly. This was something he had not bargained for. He never thought the longing for his bride would be so intense, that it phys-ically hurt to think about her. He had no traveling partner, like some on the trip had, so he had no one to talk with.

Curiously, the dog that belonged to Sasa and Coyote came around regularly, as if to say hello. Willie found himself talking to the dog, named Wheezer, on a regular basis. Sometimes, Wheezer would jump up onto the seat with him, as he drove his team of oxen. The dog sat sideways facing him and looked squarely into his eyes expectantly. After Willie told him of the day's trials and loneliness, Wheezer would bark once or twice and then jump down to run alongside the wagons. It always made Willie smile and feel just a little bit better than he had before.

Today, Wheezer had jumped up into the wagon, before coming to sit beside him on the seat.

"Well, you're a little late today Wheezer. What you been up to, that has got your coat so dirty? It looks like you've been rolling around on top of a fresh buffalo chip. I sure hope that is not what you did, but I wouldn't put it past you. Most dogs like smelly things. No reason why you should be any different. I've been thinking of my Clara today, Wheezer. I sure do miss her. She should be getting mighty big with that baby, in her belly. I hope the neighbors are taking good care of her. I know, I'm going to have to work extra hard in the gold fields to pay them back for their help.

"What's that you got on your paws? Is that blood?" asked Willie

Wheezer looked down and then moved back inside the wagon, where he could lie down to lick his feet.

"Hey, Wheezer, what's going on back there?" asked Willie.

It was unusual for Wheezer to retreat to the wagon. Willie worried about it, until the wagon train finally stopped, to rest the animals. As soon as he secured his team, he stepped back into the covered wagon and discovered Wheezer licking bloody paws.

"Here now, let me take a look at that Wheezer. What have you done to yourself?" said Willie.

Wheezer huffed and went back to cleaning his wounded paws. Upon close examination, Willie found that Wheezer's paws were sliced in several places. Probably due to the long blades of grass, that the train was passing through.

"Well, you just stay here as long as you want Wheezer. I'll tell Sasa where you are, and that your feet are injured. I imagine she will want you to ride with her in her wagon for a spell, until we get back onto short grass. This long grass can be sharp against bare skin," said Willie, as he patted Wheezer on the head.

Willie headed for Sasa's wagon, which was, several wagons away from his. As he walked he became aware of what sounded like a heated argument. He slowed his step and listened a little closer, to determine where the sounds were coming from. He came around the next wagon and quickly found the source. Two men were facing off with each other, fists were raised.

"Henley Hughes, I am tellin' you, the Wagon Master told me to run my wagon behind yours. I just do what I am told," shouted Peter Diggins.

Ever since his partner, Albert Langley died he just wanted to lay low and get to California in one piece, so he took instruction without argument. The percentage of Cherokee to whites was about even, but that meant, that somewhere in the middle of the train either a white would follow a Cherokee or the other way around. Henley had gotten more and more bombastic as the days passed and was adamant that he not have any contact with "those filthy injuns".

"I don't care who told you what. I don't trust any of you injuns to not stab me in the back, while riding behind my wagon," argued Henley.

"Then take that up with the Wagon Master. You will have to ask him to put you further ahead in the train. But, that's no call to yell at me. I run my wagon where I'm told and that's a fact. If'n you didn't want to be in a train with the Cherokees, you shoulda' not come with us. I'm sure there are other companies formin' that you coulda gone with," answered Peter.

"Now don't go telling me what I can and can't do. I go where and when I please. The government put you injuns in Indian Territory and that's where you should have to stay," replied Henley.

Just then Wheezer passed through the crowd and came forward, growling low and menacing. Henley noticed the dog and stopped talking for a moment.

"I see, you injuns would sick that mean dog on a rightful citizen of the United States. Uh, I guess I will have to have me a talk with that Wagon Master. Right about now, is as good a time as any. You just keep that dog off me, ya here?" said Henley, as he backed away.

Sasa had arrived and bent down to calm Wheezer, but he would not take his eyes from the retreating Henley. Willie Catcher patted Wheezer's head, headed back to his wagon and got back up in the seat behind his oxen.

* * * * *

Wheezer stopped his growling when Henley was finally out of sight. He knew there was something wrong about that man. He did not know what it was, but he knew that the man was dangerous and violent. He would not stand by and let any of his friends be hurt. It wasn't a Cherokee or white thing; to Wheezer they were either friends or enemies, no in between. Of course, there were people he felt closer to than others, however if you were kind and friendly, then you were a friend of Wheezer's.

After the crowd dispersed, Wheezer patrolled around a few of the resting wagons. His paws were still sore, so after once around the wagons, he headed back to Sasa's wagon and the comfy bed she had made for him.

Chapter 12

It was Saturday, May 12th and the leaders of the wagon train were sure that they would soon intersect the Santa Fe Trail. Since, they were coming at it from a new and different angle, it was hard to determine exactly when and where that would be. They knew, that the Santa Fe Trail passed by the fork of Little Turkey Creek, but no one knew what the topography looked like, coming in from the south. They were blazing this trail and making note of the land as they traveled. Later travelers would have the benefit of their writings, but for now, they could only rely on the maps they carried.

Captain Evans was preoccupied. He had not imagined that there would be so many problems crop up between the whites and the Cherokees. It did not make since to him. Having the Cherokees along helped the entire train, keep free from attack from the plains tribes. So far, there had been no violent encounters with the native tribes that roamed the very plains their wagons were traveling through. But he had to concede, that some white men could not get past their deep-seated prejudices. The Cherokees had remained non-combative during the trip, so far.

He was pleasantly pleased, that this first leg of their trip had actually cost them no lives from disease. The train had encountered no cholera or small pox, and accidents had been kept to a minimum. Only the murder of Albert Langley had marred this pleasant outlook. It occurred to him, that they might never find out who had killed Albert. The elected officials of the train were the only authority for hundreds of miles, and they were not lawmen. They were farmers, landowners and businessmen. So how would they solve this murder? It was not likely, that they would ever know, who did it or why.

*****

An ongoing argument resurfaced, on that Saturday, about the rightfulness of traveling on the Sabbath. On each occasion, the proponents of keeping the Sabbath as a day of rest were overruled. The same happened on that day, as well, so the company made night camp and prepared for a full day of travel the next day. However, on Sunday, the entire company forgot about the argument because that was the day, May 13th, in which they encountered Little Turkey Creek and the well traveled Santa Fe Trail. All rejoiced, as they made camp alongside the creek, making a special evening meal to celebrate. As soon as they had eaten, a discussion arose as to what route they would take from there. They could venture a little further north and take the Oregon Trail or stay on the Santa Fe Trail to Fort

Bent. After much heated debate, it was decided to take the Santa Fe Trail. The wagons rolled out of camp early the next morning.

It was a beautiful day, with glorious blue skies and the sun shining, making the grass glitter with the morning dew. The dew burned off quickly, as mid-morning approached. The road they had blazed, stretched out behind them to the south and the Santa Fe Trail stretched in front of them to the west.

The travelers had just completed the first ever road, running from Fayetteville, Arkansas, through Fort Smith, across Indian Territory and on through Kansas. It was a monumental achievement.

Along the way, they located a very large rock. One of the men decided this would be a fine makeshift post office. They could place their many letters under the rock, mark it for travelers going east, and eventually their letters would be carried to Independence, Missouri, where they would be deposited in the official post office. Finally, all those at home, would know that their loved ones were all in good health and continuing on to California.

During that day's travel, the company began to notice more and more dead, dried-up carcasses of cattle, that looked like they had died the previous winter. A report was noted, that the winter before had been unusually brutal and many freighters on the Santa Fe Trail, had lost most of their oxen from freezing to death. As each mile passed on the road, more and more dead cattle were observed. So many carcasses, that the live cattle, drawing the wagons, became skittish and hard to manage.

On Monday, they traveled only ten miles and during the night another fifteen head of cattle walked away from camp. Men were sent to round them up and on the next night they lost forty-five more. The whole company had helped to round this lot up. The train was at a standstill, until eight of the men returned, with the last of the cattle that they could locate. It was surmised, that the cattle got restless, because of the great amount of dead cattle on the trail.

* * * * *

Coyote helped Sasa with the biscuits for the evening meal, while she fried up some ham. Coyote had gathered some wild onions and other edible plants, while he was out scouting that day. He had even found some wild rose bushes, with last winter's rose hips still attached. He gathered all he had room for in his pouch and brought them back to camp. Many in the camp knew nothing about the need for greens in the diet and Coyote knew that if they continued to eat that way, they would eventually get sick. Rose hips and fresh green plants, kept that from happening. Sasa added the wild onions to their meal. She washed the greens and sprinkled a little vinegar and sugar over them, for a dressing. Sasa was so pleased that her husband knew so much about plants. In fact, he was even better educated, in that respect, than Sasa, even though Poison Woman herself had trained her.

For the last few days, she had worn her deerskin clothes. They seemed to wear better than the cotton dresses she owned. She changed into her skins, when she ripped the skirt of one of her tear dresses, and decided that she needed to wear something more durable.

Coyote, on the other hand, preferred to wear his blue dungarees with his deerskin shirt. The dungarees wore like iron and gave him protection against the constant rubbing of the horseflesh under him day after long day.

Both of them wore their hair in braids. It was simpler and cleaner in the long run. Especially since, there was not always water available to wash their hair in. Sasa did not like to have hair fly into her face, while she drove the team on the trail and Coyote wanted to be free of the problem of getting hair in his eyes, preventing him from seeing all that needed seeing. Both wore undecorated moccasins, with boar hide soles, that would never wear out.

*****

The man with the stolen wagon brooded. As each day passed, he knew he came one day closer to discovery. Sooner or later, Stan Grant would finally recognize him, and then his life would be over. He had to think of some way to stop that from happening. Otherwise, all that he had done to get this far, would have been for nothing at all. Why couldn't Stan have died when he had left him by the road? That was a big mistake he made, when he hadn't shot Stan again, just to be sure. Now, he was going to have to finish the job he started. But, it was hard to do, with so many people around. He would have to be very smart about it.

He had been smart when he killed that Indian, Albert. It was Albert who had somehow recognized him. He still did not know, how a Cherokee from Indian Territory would recognize a man from Arkansas, but he had and thus he marked himself for death. But, Stan would be harder to kill, because he was always with Coyote and Sasa. Those two weren't dumb Indians. Coyote scouted for the company and kept his eyes open for trouble and Sasa was an educated Indian, versed in the white man's law. She carried a gun and a knife at her side and she would protect Stan if she had to.

Then there was that dog and the coyote. They protected them all. Getting Stan alone, without those animals seeing, was going to be the hardest thing to do. But he had to find a way. One way or another, it had to be done or his prospects of succeeding were zero.

He wondered if anyone back in Arkansas missed him. It was unlikely they would ever even give him a thought. He lived alone on his place, never bothered to improve it and only had the minimum of animals; just enough to provide food for his table like eggs and chickens. No one came to visit him. No, he would not be missed and that was fine with him.

He looked down at his threadbare clothes and worn boots. Someday, he would be able to afford the best money could buy. No more accepting charity, from poor dirt farmers. He would never again have to look into the eyes of men and women, who pitied him. They used to invite him to a meal, not because he was so loved, but because he was pitied. He hated that feeling.

Chapter 13

"You know, someday soon, you men will have to make a decision. We have got to separate ourselves from the Cherokees. What do you think is going to happen when we get to the gold fields? Are you willing to let them get the best spots, instead of you? No? Well, we need to leave them far behind us. Let them eat our dust. We don't need them. Heck we ain't seen nary an Indian, except for them Osages and they was as friendly as puppy dogs. I expect it will be the same on up ahead," said Henley Hughes, as he sat around the campfire with other white men from the train.

"I think you're forgettin' that them Osages was friendly, because one of them Indians on the train knew the Chief. If'in we hadn't had them with us, it coulda turned out a mite different for us. I, for one, don't want to separate from them. I agreed to travel with them and that's what I'm agonna do," said Hiram Davis.

"Yah, and what about the Indians we is gonna come up on, as we go on west of here? Them Cherokees, is on good terms with the plains tribes, cause they had a big peace council just a few years back, I heard tell. They made peace with them and that's what I want as well. Peace. I don't want to end up with an arrow in my back, just cause you don't like travelin' with Indians, Henley. You need to stop singing that song, cause we don't want to hear it," said George Keys.

"Well, you men are goin' to remember that I gave you a chance to stop them from takin' advantage of us, oncest we get there. So don't come cryin' ta me. I plan on keepin' my gun handy and any Cherokee gets in my way in the gold fields, will be a dead Cherokee," replied Henley.

"You're just itching to make trouble, Henley. Why can't you just go along and be peaceable on this trip. None of us want trouble with the Cherokees. They've been helpful and good. They aint done nothin' to cause the kind of hate and discontent you're a spewing out. So, if'in you want anyone on this wagon to talk to ya, ya better stop the crazy talk. Yer almost foamin' at the mouth. Be careful you don't get yerself shot, for bein' rabid," said Hiram.

Henley grumbled under his breath, but did not reply. He just could not understand why these men did not see things his way. No matter, there were a few others on the train who did listen to him. He would talk to them and then maybe soon all the whites on the train would see the light and separate from them injuns. And if'in they didn't, then those Cherokees would see how the stick floats once they got to the gold fields.

*****

Dan had pulled her wagon close into the circle. By now she was adept at unhitching her team and setting them out to graze. It took less time to do it, than when she first started on the trip. However, not having someone to talk to, was beginning to get under her skin. It was easy to pretend to be a man, but keeping away from most of the other travelers, was making her very lonely.

She had watched the strange man off and on for the last few days and concluded that he was a man with secrets. But who was she to accuse anyone? She had her own secrets. But, she had a hunch that this man's secrets were dangerous to those around him, although she had no way of explaining why she felt that way.

Tonight, she saw the man cook his dinner and eat it alone inside his wagon. Later she noticed him peeking out of the back of his wagon, looking across the circle to the Cherokee portion of the train. Dan's wagon was the second Cherokee wagon in line, but the man was looking further along. She had no doubt which wagon he was interested in. It was Sasa and Coyote's wagon, and he was watching the white man that worked for them. But, why?

As she watched from behind the cover sheet of her wagon, she saw the man pull out his gun and check it for bullets. He acted like a man who was getting ready to use his gun. Then he jumped down from the wagon and disappeared into the golden dry grass surrounding the camp. This was not good. She had kept out of all the doings and relationships on the train, to maintain her anonymity. What was she suppose to do now? If she told someone, they might figure out she was a woman. Would they throw her off the train? Would she have to make her way back by herself? She didn't know, but she didn't spend much time debating it with herself. On impulse, she acted.

Now she ran past the several wagons between hers and Sasa's and arrived breathless. She located Sasa at the cook fire several feet from the wagon.

"Sasa, you don't know me. My name is Dan and I am afraid that someone is planning to hurt your white helper," said Dan.

"Oh? Why would you think that? Do you know who it is?" asked Sasa.

"I don't know his name, but he is a lone man, in a wagon, in the white part of the train. I saw him load his gun and it looked like he was headed towards your wagon," said Dan.

"Maybe he is going out to hunt. A lot of the men use this time of day to hunt," replied Sasa.

"Men don't hunt with a hand gun. They use their rifles for that. Plus, I been noticing this man and he's been watching your wagon for several days now. I can't say why, but I really think he plans on hurting one of you and I think it is your helper," said Dan.

Sasa sat straighter and began to take Dan seriously now.

"Yes, we have wondered about that man. Let me go tell Coyote, and please stay a moment and we will talk more," said Sasa.

Dan did not really want to stay any longer than necessary but it would be rude to walk back when asked to stay. So, she waited for Sasa to return.

*****

Sasa trotted around the wagon thinking she would find either Coyote or Stan on the other side. She found Stan, but not Coyote, and he was busy putting grease on the hubs of the wheels, in preparation for leaving the next day.

"Stan, can you take a minute to talk? This is important," said Sasa.

"Sure," said Stan, putting the grease bucket down and wiping his hands on an old rag.

"I just got word from someone on the train that the man we've been watching is skulking around with his handgun ready. They think he is looking for you," said Sasa.

Stan pondered for a moment.

"Who in heck would know that, Sasa? I thought, you me and Coyote were the only ones ta know about that man with the wagon. How do they know that the man is gunnin' for me?" said Stan, with a worried look on his face.

Now it was Sasa's turn to ponder. She did not want to reveal the identity of the person who raised the alarm, for her own reasons. Something was not right about Dan, but she needed time to get to the bottom of it. However, she did believe Dan's story.

"Never mind who, the person has nothing to do with you, except they observed the man watching you. Now I think..." said Sasa.

A shot rang out and a hole appeared in the cover sheet of the wagon they stood by. Stan and Sasa ducked down quickly and rolled under the wagon for protection. People on the train became alarmed, because they could not tell where the shot came from or who was doing the shooting. Chaos reigned in the camp, but no other shots were fired.

Wheezer came scurrying by the wagon, barking his irritation, then ran out into the surrounding grass.

"Wheezer, come back," cried Sasa.

But Wheezer was already gone. In a few moments Sasa could hear what sounded like Wheezer growling and yipping, then silence. Sasa and Stan waited a few more minutes before coming out from under the wagon. Just as they both stood up, Wheezer appeared with a piece of dirty white cotton, with a few specks of blood on it, in his mouth.

"I guess Wheezer found someone out there, but I bet they are long gone now," said Sasa.

"I don't doubt it. He must have scuffled with someone. But, we won't be able to tell nothin' about the person. See, it's just plain cotton. Everyone on this here train, has something made of white cotton. Thanks Wheezer, you did good, anyway," said Stan.

Sasa nodded her head, looking with concern on her face. Whoever it was, Wheezer had landed a bite. He has blood on his muzzle. Sasa removed the piece of cloth from Wheezer's mouth, petted him on the head and thanked him.

Then, Sasa remembered that Dan was waiting for her on the other side of the wagon, but when she got there Dan was gone. Sasa would have to wait to talk with Dan again and then maybe she would figure out what was bothering her about the man.

Chapter 14

Just after arriving at the Santa Fe Trail, the train met up with a wagon with four occupants.

"Ho there, the wagon," shouted Capt. Evans, as they approached the still wagon at the side of the road.

"Come alongside," one of the men in the wagon answered.

Capt. Evans halted, when his wagon came alongside the lone wagon. Evans stepped down and met one of the four men.

"Hello, I am Capt. Evans of the Evans/Cherokee Company traveling to Santa Fe and then on to California. Where are you headed?" asked Capt. Evans.

"We set off alone, instead of traveling with companies that have had disease strike them. But once we got here, we began to notice evidence of Indians about and did not want to go any further until a company came along that we could travel with. Us alone, on the prairie, makes us sitting ducks," replied the man.

"We have no disease in our company. But if you want to travel with us, I am going to have to talk with the other head of our train, James Vann," said Capt. Evans.

"That's fine, fine. We've got nothing but time. We are the Larkets from northern Missouri. All brothers who left our families waiting back home, we want to stay safe as we can, so that our families will see us again," said Mr. Larket.

Evans discussed it with Vann, who saw no problems with adding the extra wagon to the train. Four extra men could come in handy, later on. So the wagon, from Missouri, joined with the Evans/Cherokee Company.

As each day passed, the travelers found, along the trail, more and more items made of iron. Pieces that had been part of wagons and harnesses were everywhere one looked. The dead carcasses were everywhere as well, which made the remaining oxen restless and difficult to keep in camp overnight. One night, they lost so many oxen, that they did not travel for several days, until they could round them up again.

As the days went by, Sasa began to realize, that once they reached California her party of Cherokees would be the first group of Cherokees in California. The thought struck her as a little scary, conversely exciting as well. Their group of Cherokees would be making history, and who knew what would happen in the gold fields. Some of the Cherokees might come back heroes. Her thoughts were always on coming back home. Since arriving in Indian Territory, after the Trail of Tears, Sasa's goal was always to help her people grow and prosper in their new land. She had no desire to stay in California. She hoped. that all the Chero-kees would do the same, but there was no law that said they had to come back.

On May 22nd, they camped in a spot that Coyote said was an old Osage hunting party camp. No one contradicted him, because he knew the signs the Osage had left behind, a broken arrow here, and a discarded moccasin there. So, when Crawford wrote in his journal, he called it "Osage Camp", which rested on the bank of the Arkansas.

On May 26th, the men on the train hunted and came back with a live young elk, which was caught by George Keys, who just wanted to keep it overnight and let it go in the morning. The men were astonished at some of the wildlife they were seeing, that they had never seen before, such as antelopes, badgers, hares and prairie dogs, even a new kind of squirrel.

The hunters, did not have to go far from camp that day, because another huge herd of buffalo passed by them. So far, every one of the men in camp had killed a buffa-lo, except for Mr. Potter, who thought the great giants of the prairies were too beautiful to kill, unless you were very hungry. He still had plenty of stores in his wagon, so there was no need.

Everyone was looking forward to making it to Fort Mann. Fort Mann had been built in 1847 and was a small adobe station, that housed a blacksmith and a forge, to help repair the many wagons on the Santa Fe Trail, travel-ing between Independence, Missouri and Santa Fe.

On Tuesday, May 29th, they reached Fort Mann, but were disappointed to find it disserted, with over fifty empty wagons in various states of repair, all abandoned and scattered around the fort. It was a bit of a letdown, but not a catastrophe. One of the members of their train, John

Rankin Pyeatt, was a blacksmith, and he had brought all his equipment along with him. All in the party had been looking forward to meeting new people at the fort, however, it was not to be. The wagon train stopped here for about three days, while they repaired and refitted several wagon wheels that had shrunk from the dry climate. There was only two ways to fix them. One was to put the wheel into a pool of water to let it soak and swell up till it fit the rim again, or to take off the rim and let the smithy downsize it for the wheel. Each way took time.

They were ready to go by June 2nd. A decision now had to be made. There were two Santa Fe routes they could choose from. One was the "wet" route, which followed the Arkansas River and the other was the "dry" route. They chose the safer and well-watered "wet" route, which would take them to Bent's Fort, close to Santa Fe.

Then on June 4th, the train met up with traders going east from Santa Fe. They were William Guerrier and Seth Ward. Several people on the train gave the traders, more letters to their families back home. At the same time, the traders were able to advise Evans and Vann of problems up ahead and ways to avoid them.

*****

There had been no new incidents, concerning Stan, and Sasa was hoping it would stay that way. However, she knew that it had to come to a head sometime, before they reached the gold fields. Sasa was thinking of a plan to reveal that the wagon was stolen, before the going got rough on the trail. She knew, there were harder days ahead, especially, after seeing all the dead oxen on the road and abandoned wagons, and they had not reached Santa Fe yet.

Coyote and Yellow Eyes were out scouting every day and still, had not come across any signs of the tribes that

93

inhabited the area. He was vigilant in seeing that he was the first to make contact with them, if possible. He knew that, some of the men on the train's first response would be to shoot, just out of fear. But, Coyote knew most of the tribes and the sign language that would allow him to speak to them. He could stop any violence from happening, at least he hoped so.

*****

Henley had stayed quiet for the last few days. He only had a few on the train who agreed with him and he was hoping that more would change their minds, as time went on. He fantasized, that a full-scale attack from one of the plains tribes would turn them around to his way of thinking. He had only to wait for it to happen.

There were those of the white men, on the train, I do not trust. Especially, those that argued with me about the Cherokees, he thought. He had half a mind to sabotage their wagons in some way, but could not think of anything specific yet.

However, he was thinking on a new idea, one that would get rid of the Cherokees one by one, but he did not want to get caught. He would have to make sure that he was not seen.

*****

The train had stopped to camp, earlier than usual, partly because the heat was beginning to affect the oxen and mules and also because a few of the wagons reported they needed time for repairs or greasing of the wheel hubs. Coyote returned to camp with Yellow Eyes, which gave Wheezer time to play with him. They chased each other in the grass, which was now up and green, with the dry grass slumping to the ground. Wheezer could now see further and soon picked up the scent of a small animal of some kind. As he ran off in the direction of his prey, Yellow Eyes followed a pace or two behind him.

Wheezer spotted an animal he had only had glimpses of on this trip and his curiosity spiked. But, before he could get near it, the animal ducked down into its hole, disappearing from sight. Wheezer found the hole and began to vigorously claw and dig it out. Soon, the hole widened enough that he could wiggle down into it. He scooted further and further into the tunnel, with the scent of what Sasa called a "Prairie Dog" in his nose. Every bit of his hunting instinct kicked in, as he forced his way down. Finally, he reached his prey; grabbing it by the neck, he dispatched it quickly and was ready to back out of the hole. Suddenly, he heard the dirt collapse behind him and he was in complete darkness. He set the Prairie Dog down in front of him and began barking furiously.

Outside of the hole, Yellow Eyes paced frantically; the sound of Wheezer's barking raised his feeling of danger and the hair stood up on his back. Yellow Eyes was not known for his communication skills, not that he did not have them, he had, just never used them. He distrusted humans completely, except for Coyote and maybe, on a good day, Sasa. But on this occasion, he could think of nothing to do to help his friend, other than getting help. So off he ran, back to camp, where Coyote was helping Sasa with the campfire.

Yellow Eyes approached, yipping at Coyote. Then he emitted a howl, "Arooo" and ran back and forth toward the field of grass, just beyond the camp.

"What in the world is wrong with Yellow Eyes?" asked Sasa. "I have never seen him act like that before. It's like he is trying to talk to you, Coyote. You better see what is wrong; just look at the hair on his back standing up straight."

Coyote thought for a moment, debating whether to follow on foot or horse. He decided, to go on foot. He grabbed his gun and his hatchet and proceeded to follow Yellow Eyes. Coyote could barely see Yellow Eyes up ahead, but he did not lose him, then finally, Yellow Eyes came to a stop. Coyote watched his friend claw at the ground, yipping and howling. He could not think of what Yellow Eyes wanted of him, until suddenly, he heard a faint barking coming from the ground.

"I see now, Yellow Eyes. You have done a very good thing. I am very proud of you. If you had not come to get me, Wheezer would likely die down in that hole," said Coyote.

Coyote removed his knife from its sheath and began digging out the hole until he finally saw a patch of white amongst the dirt. When he removed a little more dirt, Wheezer tail popped up. As a puppy, his tail had been cropped and was just the right size to grab with a man's hand. Coyote reached down and grabbing Wheezer's tail, he proceeded to pull him out of the hole. Wheezer came out slowly, and when his head appeared, his mouth was still holding the dead Prairie Dog firmly between his jaws. Coyote began to laugh, and was still laughing, when they trotted back to camp. Wheezer set his prize at Sasa's feet, fully expecting her to eat it with him.

"I think we are going to find out what Prairie Dog tastes like. He looks like he very nearly died getting this animal and I think he wants to share it with us. But first, Coyote, you get to skin it and put it on a spit over the fire. I will tend it until it is done," said Sasa, smiling.

Chapter 15

The train continued on, and because, they received reliable information, from the traders, they knew they were headed for a splendid place called, "Big Timbers". Big Timbers received its name, for the huge cottonwood trees, that grew like an oasis on the prairie. The travelers had not seen trees for quite some time and were looking forward to the rest and shade from the intense heat, that now infiltrated the high prairie. They were told that the trees grew close to a spring fed stream, running cold from mountain runoff, and everyone was excited at the prospect.

The traders also said that this "oasis" was only about thirty miles from Bent's Fort, the next stop after Big Timbers. Anticipation was running high on the day they finally saw Big Timbers in the distance. As they rode in, they found that the trees occupied a space of about three quarters of a mile wide and about a four-mile long swath of ground. It was lush with green vegetation and abundant cottonwood trees. The traders had said, it was a common place for the Indians to winter. This made sense to Coyote who knew that the plains Indians needed some way to feed their horses during the winter, when the heavy snows covered the land. Horses could eat the twigs and bark of the cottonwood trees just fine. It was mainly the Comanche, Cheyenne, Apache and Arapahoe who wintered here, but they would be far away now, probably on a spring hunt, for buffalo, out on the plains.

There was plenty of room, for all of the wagons, to pull alongside the stream. This was a good opportunity to, refill all of the water barrels, bathe and wash clothes. All took advantage of the stream, for bathing, except for Dan, who bathed in her wagon. The women of the train all bathed together, after finding a secluded spot, with bushes, that would conceal them from prying eyes. But, Sasa found it strange, that Dan did not come down to bathe and wash his hair, when it was the men's turn. This just added to her curiosity, about the man. It was that day that Sasa found herself at the stream, where Dan was filling buckets with water for his water barrel, which gave her a good excuse to talk to him.

Sasa walked over to where Dan was scooping up water with a bucket and sat down on the sandy shore of the stream.

"Hello Dan. Isn't this a wonderful place? The water is so refreshing and cold, it absolutely renews me," said Sasa.

"Yea, I suppose it does. I need to fill my main water barrel, then I can rest," said Dan.

"Dan, don't you just want to take your boots off and stick your feet in the water? I will if you will. Come on and refresh your feet and we can talk," said Sasa.

Dan did not want to appear rude, but at the same time, she was wary of revealing any part of herself. She thought, maybe I can quickly stick my feet in and she won't see them.

Sasa just wanted an excuse to talk with Dan, so she could figure out what was bothering her about the man. But, when Dan removed his boots and quickly stuck them in the stream, Sasa was astonished at the slender form and dainty toes of Dan's feet. The water was crystal clear and Sasa could see Dan's feet very well. Quickly, Sasa removed her moccasins and stuck her feet in too and immediately noticed how much alike their feet were. Finally, an idea began to form, so that Sasa looked at Dan in a new light. Her eyes widened and she blushed faintly on her tan cheeks. The truth of the matter struck her and she was embarrassed for prying into something that Dan obviously wanted to keep secret.

What was Sasa going to do? Now that she had figured it out, what good would it do to reveal it to anyone else? Dan was not breaking any laws and it was entirely Dan's business. She decided to offer her hand in friendship. Dan must be lonely on this trip. Sasa knew, that she would be also, if she were doing the same as Dan.

"Dan, I could not help but notice your feet. I believe, I know what your secret is. I don't want to pry, but I want you to know, that you have a friend on the train. I doubt if anyone else has made the connection and I certainly won't tell anyone," said Sasa.

"Really, how can I trust you, not to tell? I don't know you and you don't know me. Why should you want to keep my secret?" said Dan.

"Because it is nobody's business, that's why. I didn't start out, to try and figure out your secret, but it just happened, when you took your boots off. One woman, can surely tell the feet of another woman. Whatever your reasons are for pretending to be a man, they are not my concern. In fact, I can understand why you're doing it. You are alone and the Wagon Master might not have accepted you in the train, if he knew. I doubt that he could do anything about it now, even if he knew. But he won't hear it from me. Will you let me be your friend?" asked Sasa.

Dan thought for a moment. She surely could use a friend and she had been so lonely.

"Alright, I guess so. But I don't want anyone to know, even when we get to the gold fields. They might not let a woman stake her own claim. I guarantee you, that I can work as hard as any man can, and I will too," said Dan.

"Is Dan short for some other name? Do you mind telling me, what your name really is?" asked Sasa.

"I suppose it won't hurt none. My name is Danica. I am Cherokee, just like you. I lost my husband and I was stuck on our farm alone. But, don't ever call me that. I don't want anyone to get any ideas about me," said Dan.

"Your secret is safe with me, Dan. You can come to me and Coyote any time you need help, or if you just want to talk and spend time visiting in the evenings. No one will think funny about that. Let's see if we can get your wagon, in line, closer to us. I can ask the Lieutenant Wagon Master that is over the Cherokee wagons. I'll say that Coyote wants it that way. They won't mind, I'm sure," said Sasa.

"That's fine, but I don't want you to tell Coyote, unless you absolutely have to. The fewer who know, the better," said Dan.

*****

The man noticed that Sasa was sitting with someone by the stream. Stan and Coyote had walked off toward the head of the train, probably to talk with Captain Evans about something. This was a great opportunity to put into action, one of his ideas, to eliminate Stan from the wagon train.

He crept along the outside of the wagons towards Coyote's wagon. The oxen had been hobbled, on the grass, a few hundred feet away. He casually walked over to the oxen, that were still wearing their harnesses. Carefully, he pulled out of his pocket a short nail that he had filed the head off of and pushed one end up under the harness of the oxen. Now when the oxen moved, the nail would make small cuts in the oxen's flesh. It would be some time before Coyote noticed it and by then the cuts would be infected. He hesitated a moment and then quickly did the same to another of the oxen, then quietly snuck away.

*****

Henley also was working on ideas he had for getting rid of the Cherokees from the wagon train. He started out from his wagon at sundown, just when it was hard to see someone clearly in the dusk. He walked to the area, where the Cherokee's wagons were circled around several cook fires. No one seemed to take notice of him and he did not draw attention to himself either.

Some of the wagons carried their water barrels on the inside of the circle and some on the outside. Henley slipped to the outside of the wagons, away from the firelight. Soon, he came to a wagon with its barrel on the outside of the circle. He stealthily removed the round lid from the barrel and dropped in a large handful of saltpeter. This would make the water taste very salty and a bit bitter. If the occupants of that wagon did not check their water before they left Big Timbers, they would not have drinkable water, until they stopped near water again.

His tactic was not life threatening, but he had decided to start with small nuisances first and step up the dirty tricks, if the Cherokees continued with the train. He succeeded in salting four of the wagons, owned by the Cherokees. He was happy he did not meet up with that dog and coyote that belonged to one of the Cherokee wagons. He walked back to his wagon, satisfied he had done a good nights work.

*****

The train stayed in Big Timbers a few days and once repairs were completed, the company prepared to move on. James Vann took a ladle from the side of his wagon and dipped it into his water barrel for a long draught. Suddenly, he spit the water out.

"Something is wrong with my water! I just filled the barrel two days ago and it should be sweet, not salty. This is undrinkable!" said James, to the owner of the next wagon. "This isn't right! I suspect sabotage to my water barrel. Everyone, before we leave here, check your water barrels.

Many drivers grumbled at the nuisance of checking their barrels, but were happy they did, when they found three other barrels were contaminated. James walked over to Coyote, who was already on his horse and ready to begin his scouting for the day's travel.

"Coyote, would you please head up to the front and tell Capt. Evans that we must delay for about an hour. Explain that our water has been tampered with and we must dump these barrels and refill them with new water. I will send word when we are ready," said James.

Coyote nodded, turned his horse around and headed for the front of the train. With others helping out, it took less than an hour to fill the four water barrels and the train was ready to go soon after. The whites on the train checked their water also, but found that only the Cherokees water barrels had been tampered with.

Chapter 16

Since finding the Santa Fe Trail, the soil had become increasingly drier. The old grass from the year before, became much shorter and the weather much hotter. Every turn of the their wheels, kicked up dust, sand and small rocks, as they went. The last part of the train, choked on the dust, kicked up by the wagons that went before them. Most kept a bandana or piece of cloth tied around their faces, to filter out the unbreathable particles in the air. They were following, what is known as the "Mountain Route", which ran as closely as possible to the Arkansas River.

The Evans/Cherokee Company had no way of knowing, that they were virtually at the head of a long line of other companies following behind them, the first of which, was only about fifteen miles back. Those companies had come out of Independence, Missouri and had already experienced much disease and hardship. But for the Evans group, their way was easier, because they were first to the new grasses that were greening the landscape all around them and the watering stops had not been fouled, by multitudes of other travelers.

Sasa and Stan continued to switch duties, so that no one had to drive the team of oxen an entire day. They saw little of Coyote, until he returned in the afternoon, just before they made camp. One of Coyote's duties was to find a suitable stopping place, for the more than forty wagons in the train.

Coyote had his own problems though, as any scout would. He was always looking out, for signs of his people. So far, there had been none; in fact they had only met up with a small party of four Indians, since they met the Osages back on the Cherokee Trail. What Coyote did see, was sign of large numbers of travelers, probably Indians, at various places along the Arkansas River. Recently vacated campsites and water crossings, were obvious to him. He wondered where all these Indians were headed, but he did not see any other scouts or advance parties along the way.

The day had been abnormally muggy, with a thunderhead far off in the distance. Most had ignored the signs of an oncoming storm on the prairie, which then took them all by surprise. The storm began with high winds, which rocked the wagons enough that the Wagon Master called a halt and they formed their wagons into circles, as they had in the past. But, before they got down from the wagons, huge hail began to fall. Each person had to take refuge, many of them under their wagons. A few injuries were sustained, from the hard-hitting balls of ice, as it rocketed out of the sky. Soon, the prairie was covered white, which resembled lumpy snow. Several wagons were damaged, which required the train to camp for the night, while repairs were made and wagon sheets were sewn, where the hail had rent them.

Sasa sat in the wagon as she sewed the holes shut in the wagon sheeting, when Coyote stepped up to join her. Sitting next to her, he stayed quiet, until finally he spoke.

"Sasa, I have seen sign of many people traveling on the prairie. They are headed south from here, as far as I can tell. I'll bet that there is a large council being held on the prairie. That would explain, why we have not seen very many hunting parties or encampments along the way," said Coyote.

"I don't suppose it means anything for us, does it? I guess we don't have to worry about them now, do we?" asked Sasa.

"No, but things might be different for us, on our way back home. I was expecting this trip to be much harder than it has been, but so far, we are doing well. We have had no illness, to speak of. Other than the evil incidents directed at Stan and the murder of Albert, there have been few problems. I am not sure who tainted the water back at Big Timbers, but I have an idea. The tension between the races is my biggest concern now," said Coyote.

Sasa reached up and moved a stray lock of hair from in front of Coyote's eyes. She placed her small hand on the side of his face and held it there for a time. Looking into his deep brown eyes, she smiled.

"I am so proud of you, Coyote. My heart is ready to burst, with love for you. You are a good man and I am happy to be your wife. I am on this trip to be with you, not for the gold, so, when you say it is time to head back that is when we will go," said Sasa, as tears trickled down her tan face.

It puzzled Coyote that she would find reason to cry. It was not like her to be so emotional. Usually, she was a rock of strength, but lately she seemed more vulnerable, softer and loving. He did not know much about women, except for his own mother, but he had never seen his mother behave like this.

However, Sasa had a secret and she would not tell Coyote, until the time was right. Too many things were happening on the train that, so far, been unexplained. She felt she needed to get to the bottom of the mystery, before revealing to Coyote what she knew to be true.

*****

The hailstorm did little damage to Dan's wagon, but she was upset all the same. Ever since the episode at Big Timbers, where Sasa guess her secret, she was beside herself with worry. She did not know Sasa very well. They had lived in different parts of the Cherokee Nation, so, she was not sure she could trust Sasa. She imagined many different scenarios of what might happen, if the Wagon Master found out that she was a woman. Most were purely fantasy, but it heightened her anxiety as each day passed.

She was winding up some rope that had come loose from the side of her wagon, when Peter Diggins walked over and pulled up a small barrel; sitting down he heaved a sigh of relief.

"Well, I finally got all my repairs made. Now, I can rest a mite, before I start my fire to make dinner. Whatcha been doing, today? I find it is pretty lonely, drivin' by myself, day after day. I'm missin' Albert a heap. We brought food enough for two, so if'in you need anythin', just ask me. I even got plenty of soap too. Hey, you wanta share a fire tonight? We both are cookin' for one; it might make it easier on both of us," said Peter.

Dan was astonished. No man had approached her, even to be friendly and she had found comfort in that. However, here was Peter, trying to be a friend. How should she react...? The only thing she could do was to be as normal as possible.

"Sure, that sounds like a good idea to me. I'm not done with my repairs just yet, but I will holler at you as soon as I am ready to start my fire," said Dan.

Peter was uncommonly happy about striking up a friendship with this small man. He didn't know much about him, except that he kept to himself, never complained and worked hard. But, there was something about him that Peter, could not pin down. It drew him in and caused him to beg an acquaintance. But Peter did sense that there was something hidden about Dan. Maybe, if they became friends, he would find out what it was.

*****

Wheezer roamed among the wagons, after the hailstorm, listening to the various conversations. Occasionally, he would receive a pat on the head or even a small piece of meat. He only accepted meat from those he knew were friends, especially, those who let him hunt for vermin in their wagons. He finally came to Stan's stolen wagon and began to walk past, when the crack of a whip sounded like a shot from a gun. Pain shot through his body.

"You get your miserable hide away from my wagon. Go on! Get, before I cut you into little pieces," said the man.

Wheezer crouched down to defend himself, if needed, baring his teeth at the man. He knew full well, who this man was. He was an enemy, not a friend. Just as quickly, one of the other wagon drivers ran up to the man and grabbed his whip out of his hand.

"What in tarnation are you doin'? Wheezer is a member of this train. He was just walkin' by. You had no call to whip him. Wheezer works for his way, too. He kills the mice and rats that get into our wagons to ruin our food. He does more for the train than you do. I have half a mind to use this whip on you," said David Markle.

David was from Arkansas, near Fayetteville, where he tanned hides for a living. He had strong arms and a robust body and could have easily backed up his words, if needed.

Sensing that he had drawn attention to himself, which he did not want, he nodded and without asking for his whip, stepped back up into his wagon, where he stayed. David just shook his head, threw the whip on the ground and went over to Wheezer to check for any wounds.

Wheezer was happy to be defended by a friend, but the whip had stung him on his back and it still hurt. A little bit of blood seeped from the wound. David had been chewing some tobacco, so he took a lump from his mouth and placed in on Wheezer's wound. Immediately the hurt began to subside and Wheezer was grateful.

"Now don't you worry none, I won't let that man do that again. I'll keep an eye out for ya, if'n you want. It might be best if you steered clear of him. Ok, Wheezer?" said David.

* * * * *

Unknown to David and Wheezer, Stan had been close by and had watched all that transpired. He bristled at what the man had done to Wheezer, but he hesitated to do anything about it. It was not part of their plan, to confront this man yet. But, this time Stan got a better look at the man, and although he still could not identify him, he did find that something about him was familiar. That meant that Stan must have met him, sometime in the past. If he could only remember, it would help them when they confronted the man, to take back Stan's wagon. But, try as he might, he just could not think of where he had seen this man before. The man still wore his hat, pulled down close on his head, which shaded his face. Plus, Stan thought that if he did know this man, it was not in the style of clothes the man wore now.

Stan backed off and returned to Sasa's wagon. He reported the wounding of Wheezer to her and also his conclusions about the man. By that time, Wheezer had also returned to the wagon and Sasa took a little time to check on Wheezer's wound. It may be that she would have to go and talk to this man herself, but not unarmed, or alone. She felt this man was very dangerous. He had already tried to kill Stan, when he stole his wagon, so that meant, that he was capable of killing anyone.

Chapter 17

The skies cleared and the next morning the train headed west, still on the Santa Fe Trail. It was a short two days, till they reached Bent's Fort. It had never been a military fort, but was built for protection, as well as for business. Regular visitors to the fort were mountain men, trappers, soldiers, entire Indian camps and immigrants, like those on the Evans/Cherokee train.

A visitor to the fort had written a description back in 1839:

Round towers pierced for cannon, command the sweep all around the building, the walls are not less than fifteen feet high.... there are the storerooms, the extensive wagon houses, in which to keep the enormous heavy wagons used twice a year to bring merchandise from the States, and to carry back the skins of the buffalo and the beaver.... the great wall encloses numerous separations for domestic cattle, poultry, creatures of the prairie, caught and tamed, blacksmith and carpenter shops.

Another writer's description said:

Bent's Fort lies on the left (North) bank of the Arkansas, close by the river, and is the finest and largest fort, which we have seen on this journey. The outer wall is built of imperfectly burnt brick; on two sides arises two little towers with loopholes. In the ample courtyard were many barn-yard fowl...they have cattle, sheep and goats, and three buffalo calves, that peacefully graze with the rest of the herd. At the time they had no superfluity of horses...a band of Indians had driven away a hundred head.

The train pulled their wagons along the riverbank. While Capt. Evans and James Vann went inside the fort, the immigrants began to make camp. On this day, Robert Bent along with his many workers, were busy pressing buffalo hides that had recently come in from the various Indian tribes of the plains. Mr. Bent took time out, to make them feel welcome.

Robert Bent wiped his hands on a rag and came around the pressing table to greet his guests. He wore a dirty cotton shirt, deerskin pants and a buffalo leather apron.

"Well I'll be, hornswoggled. I've had lots of travelers come through here, but you are the most unique. Who'd a thought that the Cherokee would band together with whites from Arkansas, to go to the gold fields of California. This calls for a bit of a celebration. Would the leaders honor me at my table this evening? We've got a good buffalo hump roast and all the fixins. Your wagons are welcome to set up camp and the supply store will be open in the mornin', bright and early, afor you leave. We just got in a supply barge, sent up the river from Westport, Missouri last week, so we have almost everything in stock," said Robert, while he shook the hands of Capt. Evans and James Vann.

"We most certainly will be happy to accept. We'll just get cleaned up some before we come. I also have a very good Lakota scout and his Cherokee wife that I would like to invite to dinner, if you don't mind. We have some important questions for you and he would especially benefit from your answers. He may even have some questions for you himself. He is fluent in English," said Capt. Evans.

"Fine, fine, we have room at the table. My brothers, Charles and George, are out hunting for stray horses, so it will just be my family and me tonight. Even Kit Carson is away, on a scouting job for the military. So bring them along. It will be most interesting to meet them," said Robert.

That night, Sasa was amazed at the layout of the dining table. It had a starched white tablecloth, set with fancy china and silverware, fit for any dinner in the east. She wore one of her best Cherokee tear dresses and Coyote wore his Lakota designed skins. This would be the first time that Coyote had been invited to a dinner party, other than the Halley's dinning room. He was careful to remember all that Sasa had taught him about table etiquette, surprising Robert Bent.

After a sumptuous dinner, they were served a sweet after dinner wine, while they talked of pertinent matters.

"One of our questions, Robert, is that of finding a guide at our next stop. That will be Pueblo, in Mexican Territory. We need someone to guide us through the mountains," said Capt. Evans.

"Well, once you reach Pueblo, you will be approached by various mountain men, claiming to be guides. Not all of them are trustworthy. I know a man, Dick Owens, who lives there and used to travel with Fremont. He is also a good friend of Kit Carson. He owns some property that he farms there. If he is available, he would make a good guide.

He used to be a mountain man and he knows those mountains," said Robert.

Coyote nodded, taking in the bit of information, for later use. The dinner ended late in the evening, with a good time had by all. The train stayed at Bent's a couple of days, then, continued on the trail toward Pueblo. By the time the train pulled into Pueblo, many of the wagons had wheels that had shrunk up so badly, they could not go any further without repairs. Capt. Evans and James Vann used the time to look for a guide. However, a disagreement was brewing within the company.

Sasa had gone to the local general store for some supplies and on her way back, she encountered a large group of men, from the village, talking with several men from the train. She could not think of what they might have to discuss, so she stopped to listen.

"Seniors, you cannot take wagons through the mountains. It is just not possible; there is no wagon road wide enough to take a wagon. You will be stranded, your stock will die and you will lose all you goods. Anyone in their right mind knows, that you can only use pack horses or mules to make it through," said one of the villagers.

"Are you sure? We've heard nothing about that, not even at Bent's Fort. Now, all of a sudden we can't use our wagons? This makes no sense. Where will we get pack mules? What do we do without wagons and supplies?" said Peter Diggins.

"I am sure you will be able to sell your wagons and whatever supplies you can't pack, to any number of villagers, if you ask around. As for mules and such, I have some for sale and also a few others have some. There might be enough to supply you, if you decide to pack," said the villager.

That night in camp the discussion heated up. Some of the Cherokees had decided that packing through the mountains would be best and were ready to sell off their gear and supplies. But some argued that the villagers were liars, trying to make a quick dollar off of travelers that didn't know any better. The arguments went on for a few more days. James Vann had finally decided that packing was the best way to go and was already making arrangements for mules in the village. Others followed suit, so that at least ten wagons were sold off for pack animals.

The men and women, who had decided to take their wagons, just shook their heads when one of the packers sold his wagon for only five dollars and basically gave away most of the supplies he could not pack.

Four wagons decided they had had enough and headed back to Indian Territory. But the fact still remained, that the thirty or more wagons going on, had not found a guide as yet. They would be taking a completely different route. One that had never been traversed by wagons before and they needed a competent guide.

Sasa and Coyote tried desperately to convince a few of the Cherokee to keep their wagons and go with them. Packing through the mountains was going to be very dangerous. But nothing she said made any difference to them. Stan Grant was happy to be gong with the wagon train, because the man with the stolen wagon was also staying with the train. Stan was determined to get his wagon back and expose the thief. Now they waited for Capt. Evans to find a guide.

*****

The man sat and pondered what his next move might be. The likelihood of Stan finding out who he really was had increased, with the elimination of at least ten wagons from the train. But, he had to keep up the disguise as long as possible. Maybe Stan would never figure it out. Why could they not have gone with the packers? Several of the Cherokee were going to pack and it would have been natural for that Cherokee, Sasa, to go with them. He had been surprised that Sasa had elected to stay with the train, instead.

So far, all of his warnings had gone unheeded. The only thing left was to kill Stan Grant, but he did not think the timing was right. Better he wait for them to be isolated on the trail, before he figured out a way to do it. Sooner or later, he would have his chance and he would get rid of Stan and maybe Stan's friends, as well.

＊＊＊＊＊

Henley sat next to his wagon brooding. He had wanted to sell his wagon and pack, but he refused to go with so many of the Cherokees. He had wanted to find a way of getting rid of them from the train, but he wanted them to go home to Indian Territory, not keep going to the gold fields. Now he was stuck with his wagon, going a way that wagons had never gone before. And there were still Cherokees on the train.

It was said, that they would have to cross a terrible desert, but few knew what they might encounter. From Pueblo they would head north towards the Great Salt Lake. They might even meet some of the Mormons, who have taken refuge there, away from the U.S. Army and the people of various states, that they were forced to leave. At least, they were not Indians. He continued to stew over the fact, that there were still Indians on the wagon train and he was forced to travel with them. He may yet, find a way, to rid the wagon train of them.

He had managed to become friendly with others in the wagon train, which, were from the same area of Arkansas, as he was. Many of the travelers had banded together in groups, either by family or by the county they were from. This made things a little harder, because some of these

115

groups wanted things their own way, such as observing Sunday Sabbath. That argument had been going on for some time and it looking like it might come to a head soon. He did not care one way or the other. His only, real concern, was sharing any of his gold, with Indians.

*****

The night before the packers and train split to go their separate ways, it was unseasonably mild and the stars came out in abundance. Dan sat at the back of her wagon wondering, if she had made the right decision. She had wanted to go with the packers, but such close proximity to the others and the lack of privacy, made it impossible for her to choose that means of travel. She would have to stay with the train and the other Cherokees. For the first time, she was worried that her plan was not well thought out and it might be subject to failure.

One bright light in the situation was that Sasa, her new friend, was staying with the wagon train and she did not have to keep her secret around her. She also had developed a new friendship recently. One that she did not seek out, for herself, but that had just happened. Peter Diggins seemed to always be around to help and never asked questions of a personal nature. He was an easy person to like, so Dan did not shy away from spending time with Peter. She had to remember, that Peter thought Dan was a man and she must do nothing to make him think otherwise. There was still so far to go and many perils to overcome. She hoped that her efforts were not doomed to fail.

Chapter 18

The packers were ready to depart, when they learned that a certain Army lieutenant, who had been called to California, wanted to join them. He was Lieutenant Alfred Pleasanton and he was accompanied by ten of his men from the 2nd Dragoons. This gave the packers a bit more confidence, about their trip, where safety was concerned. However, it was the lieutenant that desired to go with the packers, because they had a competent guide in Dick Owens.

Their route led them north to the South Platte River and from there, they would follow the South Platte, until they reached Fort St. Vrain. At St. Vrain, they crossed the South Platte River and continued northwest, intersecting the Cache la Poudre River, then, heading west to the Green River.

One of the packers, James Gavin, became ill, so by the time they reached the Green River, the packer company was forced to build a skin raft to carry him across. They also loaded several packs in the make-shift boat.

"James, this should hold, to get you across. I will tie a rope on the saddle of my mule, to help pull you across. Just lay still," said one of the men.

James was so sick, that he was unable to use a paddle to help himself across.

The river was running swiftly and there was no place for an easy crossing. As some of the packers led their reluctant animals into the water, others were trying to coax the skin boat with James reclining in the center, to float toward the other shore.

Suddenly, the current began to swirl around in circles and the water splashed up on the sides, the boat began to jerk with each pull from the swimming mule. The boat and the mule were now out in the deepest part of the river, when James began to cry out.

"Hey, I'm taking on water. What do I do?" cried James.

No one could get to him at this point, because everyone was swimming across. Suddenly the sides of the skin boat collapsed, folding in on itself and James Garvin and the packs were sucked underwater, never to rise again. The swimming mule could not pull the boat once it sunk, so its swimming owner, untied the rope before the mule drowned.

Everyone else made it safely across but the packs of Hiram Shores, Aaron Tyner, and the Morrow boys were lost, as well as James Garvin. The packers gathered to say a word over James' watery grave, before continuing on.

* * * * *

After thoroughly searching, they never found a guide. So, the Evans/Cherokee Company made ready to leave anyway. They had acquired eighteen wagons and their occupants in Pueblo and all were excited to again be on the move. From Pueblo, they headed due north and begin an ascent from

4,660 feet elevation to 7,520 feet. It would be harder on the animals, so they would have to allow them more rest time. The route they were taking was called The Trapper's Trail and it had been used by trappers and mountain men for years. These would be the first wagons on this trail.

Sasa found the travel harder than the first leg of the trip, so, she let Stan take the job of driving the wagon when she got tired. Coyote was still scout for the train and he seemed more familiar with the terrain than before. Part of this route was the same one he had traveled on his journey from his people in the north.

It had been a dry, blisteringly hot day and the animals struggled with the upward climb and the higher elevation. Others on the train were having the same problem and stops to rest the animals, were called often. It was at one of the rest stops, that Sasa found herself in desperate peril. The wagon master had stopped the train along a bluff that hovered over the river. It was the flattest ground he could find, but because the bluff was a shear drop to the water, they could not let the animals lose from their harnesses. So Sasa brought water to her oxen in buckets, climbing down to the water time and again to give all of them a long drink.

Wheezer made each trip with her to the river and back. On the last trip, she placed her feet carefully, until she stepped on something soft and moving. It was too late by the time she heard the rattle of the snake at her feet and before she knew her situation, she was bitten. Just as quickly, Wheezer grabbed the snake and shook it, until its neck was broken. Then for good measure, he picked it up and did it again.

The shock of it caused Sasa to fall on her side and slide down to the water's edge. No one was around and Coyote was away from camp. Quickly, she pulled her knife from its sheath at her side. She sat up and immediately found the bite on the side of her calf, just above her high-top moccasin. She ripped a strip from the bottom of her underskirt and she deftly sliced into her leg, cutting through the bite from side to side and vertically as well. Blood came gushing over her calf pooling on the ground under her, but she paid it no mind.

Wheezer was barking at the snake, daring it to try it again. Sasa allowed the cuts to flow freely for a time, then, she washed it off with river water and bound her leg with the cloth. Each step up the steep bank was excruciatingly painful. She tried to use her arms, to pull herself up the terrain, rather than her legs. She knew that using her legs was causing the poison to pump through her body. She rested, lying on her belly; face down before continuing up the grade. Finally, she made it to her wagon, limping, when Stan noticed her.

"What in tarnation have you done, Sasa? You look like death warmed over," said Stan.

"I've been bitten by a rattler. Please come to the wagon and help me. I have some things in that wooden box, under the flour sack, that I need," said Sasa.

Stan obliged by removing the flour sack to bring her the wooden box.

"Now, I am going to ask for some things in the wagon. Please, do it as quickly as possible. I will need bacon grease from our morning breakfast. It is stored in that crock with the cloth tied over the top. Then, I need a handful of corn meal," said Sasa.

Once Stan delivered the items, she took a tin cup and added the grease and corn meal together. Then from the box, she took out two bags. Each contained a powder made from bloodroot and black cohosh. The box belonged to Coyote and was where he stored his herbal medicines. Coyote had learned the art of healing from the medicine man, of the Lakota, and kept its contents up to date and fresh.

Sasa mixed the ingredients and was about to apply it to her leg, when Coyote rode up to the resting train. He noticed right away that something was wrong. He jumped from his horse and ran to Sasa. Without a word, he saw what she was attempting to do, so he took over the chore of applying the poultice.

"Now Stan, you need to build a fire and boil some water. I have to make a tea for her to drink and it can't wait until we camp. Then go to the head of the train and let the wagon master know, that we will be delayed. He can go on if he wants and we will catch up, but we must take care of this now," said Coyote.

Stan ran to obey, but he was doubtful that Sasa would live through this. He had never seen anyone who was bit by a rattler live. The wagon master drove the train on another five miles, then, they made camp.

Coyote poured water into a pot and brought it to a boil. To the water he added some of the herbs Sasa had used in the poultice and a couple others as well. When the mixture had steeped enough, he poured off a cupful and gave it to Sasa to drink.

"I know it is hot, but try to drink it as hot as you can stand it. The hotter the better," said Coyote.

The concern and love that showed in his eyes alerted Sasa to how serious this bite was. He insisted she drink two cups of the brew, before they packed up and headed for the wagon train. Coyote changed the poultice twice in route.

"Usually, a rattler bite will cause the flesh to rot, but if we keep this up and change it regularly, we should avoid that. Do you need anything for the pain? I have something in my box, but it will put you to sleep," said Coyote.

Sasa was gritting her teeth from the pain. All she could manage was a nod of her head. Tears began to form in the corner of her eyes, from the effort to be brave. The pain made it hard for her to be strong. However, Coyote added the pain-relieving herbs to her second cup. Soon she was sound asleep, curled up on the tarps, at the back of the wagon. Wheezer brought the dead snake to Coyote, to show him he had killed it and received a fond caress.

Even though Sasa was asleep she began to sweat profusely, soaking her calico dress, but she slept on. Coyote did not want to be caught alone by any of the tribes in the area, so he gave Stan a cloth and a bucket of cold river water, so that he could sit with her and put cool compresses on her forehead.

Coyote, Stan and Wheezer arrived by nightfall, with Sasa in the back of the wagon. The wagon master allowed the train to stop for two days, while Sasa hovered between life and death. At the end of two days, Coyote examined the wound very carefully, before making his decision on what to do next.

"Sasa, the wound looks like it is trying to heal some, but I have got to keep the flesh from getting infected. I believe the poison is gone now, but you could lose your leg if we don't do something now. It will require you to be very brave," said Coyote.

"I trust you Coyote. I will do whatever it is you want, my love," said Sasa.

Coyote had built up a good fire for their evening meal, so he put the end of his knife into the flames and rested the handle on a rock, while it heated. Next, he went over to Sasa, removed the poultice from her leg and cleaned the wound well. He gave Sasa a thick piece of rawhide, to put in her mouth, to clamp down on. He got up, went to the fire and returned with his knife, holding the grip with a piece of leather. Before Sasa could lose her nerve, Coyote pressed the tip of the red hot knife on the wound, allowing it to rest there for a few seconds, while the skin hissed and sizzled. The stench of burned flesh arose from her leg, when Coyote removed the knife. By that time, Sasa had passed out. It would be several days, before she would be able to walk.

Chapter 19

The man with the stolen wagon, had not planned on Sasa' accident or it causing the train to rest, for two days. He wanted the train to keep moving, so that an opportunity could present itself to accomplish his goal. He had planned on, getting rid of Stan Grant and preventing him from discovering who he really was. The train was now headed due north and following an established trail.

One good thing was, that Stan was so busy helping Sasa, that he had no time to wander around the camp, plus, the new thirteen wagons, which, had just joined them, made it easier to blend in again.

But, he still worried about what he would do, if Stan confronted him. Why did things have to happen this way? Why, was he plagued by this man, who should by all rights be dead? He was entitled to the gold, as much as any man, wasn't he? But with every turn, things seemed to pop up to entangle him and trip him up. He promised himself, that he would not let anything stop him, especially, since he had given so much up just to be here on this trip. He was sure, that the folks back home were wondering why he had not been around lately. Well, let them wonder. He didn't care if he ever saw any of them again.

*****

Coyote was worried about Sasa, but he had other things bothering him as well. When the train moved out, Coyote settled in the seat to drive the oxen. Temporarily relieved from his scouting, he had more time to think. He opened the pouch that hung around his neck, pulling out the chain and cross that he had found on the floor of Albert's wagon. He had shown the cross and chain to Peter Diggins, who had been Albert's partner going to the gold fields. But, Peter did not recognize it at all and said, he had never seen Albert wear anything like it.

Coyote began to wonder if the chain and cross belonged to Albert's murderer. But, it still told him nothing. Many people were religious and considered themselves Christians, but there was something about the cross and chain that made him think, that it was special to the owner in some way. He slipped it back into his medicine bag and continued to drive the oxen.

Stan and Wheezer rode in the wagon watching Sasa, while Yellow Eyes sat up next to Coyote. While Sasa recuperated, they passed a creek called Fontaine Quibouille. Thus named, because of the way it boiled up from the spring. They could see Pike's Peak which had been forty miles away, but looked like they could reach it in an hour. They came into a high pine forest, which was called The

Black Forest, for the way the dense Ponderosa pine trees looked from a distance. Then they came to Cherry Creek, an offshoot from the South Platte River, which was named for the wild Choke Cherries that grew along its banks.

On an overcast day, they reached Fort St. Vrain, which had been an important trading post in times past. It was now, deserted and in shambles. Capt. Evan approached Coyote, when they made camp.

"Well Coyote, ahead are the South Platte and then, the Cache la Poudre rivers. If we keep going north, we shall have to cross both. But, I believe that the two rivers meet, not very far, east of here. If we build us a ferry boat, we can float each wagon to the confluence and then only have to cross the South Platte," said Capt. Evans.

"That would take a fairly good sized boat to handle the wagons, sir, and many days. Can we spare the time?" asked Coyote.

"The time does not bother me as much as the materials we need to build it. I don't want to have to unload the wagons to ferry them. We have trees along the river, but I don't think they are big enough," said Capt. Evans.

"Why don't we use the timbers left over from Fort St. Vrain? And there is enough pines here, we can get all the pitch we need from them. Once we put each wagon on, it only needs to float past the confluence and to the other shore. We can move it with ropes, poles and paddles," suggested Coyote.

Coyote's people were familiar with making boats to cross rivers of all sorts. He just needed some instruction on the size it needed to be and the other men on the train could help build it.

Soon, everyone on the train was involved in building the ferry boat. It would take several days to ferry all the wagons and animals across. The distance from Fort St. Vrain's and past the confluence, turned out to be seventeen miles. Each time the boat returned to Fort St. Vrain, they loaded it with as much as it could hold. Sometimes, just a fully loaded wagon, other times several oxen with men to keep them calm and steady. The boat was built so well, that once everything was across the river, they left the boat on the north side, so that others could use it. The train now headed west. The company could see the beautiful Rocky Mountains in the distance.

Now they were going up the Cache la Poudre River and once again the Cherokees were blazing the trail, this was a wagon road that others could use, all without a guide.

After following the Cache la Poudre River, they came to a fork in the river. One river was going northwest and one was going north. An explorer named Fremont had been through this route in 1843 and had written down, that he had taken the north fork of the river. Capt. Evans decided they should follow suit.

Sasa was now well enough to drive the team, for short intervals, before Stan took over for her. This gave Coyote time to continue his scouting duties. Each day the men of the train were required to help cut down brush and small trees or other obstacles to their progress. It made for slow going, some days. Along the way, they came across red buttes and precipices, with high rolling country. The Black Hills continued on, until finally, they crossed into the Laramie Plains.

They never seemed to be out of sight of buffalo, and wild game was plentiful. Everyone's larders were well stocked with meat. Now, they were traveling northwest across the Laramie Plains and they could see one end of the Medicine Bow Mountains.

It was Saturday, July 14th and some in the party wanted to spend the Sabbath by the flow of the North Platte River. But, Coyote had scouted ahead and could see a darkening in the sky, to the north, and that meant that the North Platte would swell from rainfall, making it impossible to cross. So, by Sunday afternoon, they all were across the river and headed northwest toward the Laramie Mountains.

*****

Henley Hughes sat at his fire, as the day came to an end. They had drawn the wagons into a double circle, with a community fire in the middle. He could see across the wide circle, the wagons of the Cherokees and fumed that he had not thought of anythin' to get rid of them. Nothin' had come to him, except outright murder and he would not do that. He would be found out too easily if'n he tried that. He still had a few friends that chafed at the thought of Indians on the train, but they were too lily-livered to try anythin'.

Then an idea came to him. He would have to do it at night, but if he was real quiet he could accomplish it. Once he was finished, he would melt back into the night, to his own wagon, unseen.

That night, after everyone was bedded down and sleeping, Henley crept toward the wagons of the Cherokees. There weren't as many as at the beginnin', but there was still quite a few. He started with the first one he came to. Havin' come alongside the wagon, he found the first wheel, in the dim light, of the dying fire. He reached for the linchpin that held the wagon wheel onto the axel and quickly removed it, then on to the next wheel. He put the pins in his pocket and moved to the next wagon. After he had altered three of the wagons, he was reachin' for the linchpin of the forth and suddenly he heard a ferocious growl. He looked up and saw the fire reflected in the searin' eyes of a wild coyote, Wheezer's friend, Yellow Eyes. Slowly, he backed away, without turnin' around and once he was halfway across the circle, ran to his wagon. It was amazin' that the coyote had not followed him.

*****

Off to the side, Dan had been watching. Dan had not been close enough to see what Henley had done to the wagons, but she knew that Henley was up to no good. Something was not right and she knew something must be done. But she did not want to draw attention her to herself. How could she help, without becoming the center of attention? She decided to wait until morning, then, decide what to do.

Dan went back to her wagon. Henley had not gotten to her wagon, before Yellow Eyes had stopped him, so, she knew, that whatever sabotage had been done, it did not affect her wagon. She crawled up and lay down on the bed of blankets inside, staring up at the stars, with her wagon sheet down. She thought of all the things she gave up, to be here, now. She missed wearing a nice dress and combing her long hair. She missed the touch of her husband and staying in one place. The gold did not glitter so brightly now, but she was locked into her plan, with no way to turn around. Tears flowed from her eyes, as she cried silently. Maybe tomorrow would be a better day.

*****

Peter Diggins also lay awake in his wagon. He had not heard Henley take the linchpins from his wheels. He was busy thinking about Dan. He knew something about Dan, but didn't dare say. He knew it must be kept secret and he did not know what Dan might do, if he revealed what he knew. His heart ached for the turmoil it would cause, if he opened his mouth. He did not know, what might happen to Dan if anyone knew the secret. He closed his eyes to a fitful sleep.

Chapter 20

The day began like any other on the trail. The sun came up in a glorious blaze, heralding, that the day would be hot. The fires had already been started for the morning biscuits and people were getting the harness and tack ready for the day. They were planning to try and find a way through the South Pass of the mountains, but the evening before, the scouts had returned saying that the pass was not possible. There was too much blocking the way. So today, they would follow the North Platte again, then, go around Sheep Mountain. Crossing the divide between the Atlantic and Pacific, also known as the Great Divide, was still ahead.

*****

Sasa loved the smell of fresh cooked bacon in the morning. It seemed everyone was frying up a good sized slab of it today. She had sat down to begin eating her quick breakfast, when Dan joined her.

"Good morning Sasa. Did you sleep well?" asked Dan.

"I did, but I think Wheezer and Yellow Eyes were up most of the night. It was very early in the morning, before they settled down in their beds," said Sasa.

"Sometimes other people can keep one up, if they make enough noise," said Dan.

"I didn't hear anything in particular last night, but then, dogs and coyotes have much better hearing that we do. At least, it seems that way to me," said Sasa.

Dan drew closer to Sasa, so that she could speak low.

"I was up late last night. I couldn't sleep. I was walking by the wagons and I saw something that was very strange," said Dan.

"What was it, Dan?" asked Sasa.

"I saw Henley Hughes fiddling with the wagons. The suspicious thing is, he was doing something only to the Cherokee's wagons. But, when he came to your wagon, Yellow Eyes caught him and Henley backed off and went back to his wagon. Sasa, I don't want anyone to know that it was me who saw this, and you know why. But, I felt you needed to know. I am sure he was up to no good," said Dan, anxiously.

"Can you tell me which wagons?" said Sasa.

"For sure, the three wagons, just before yours. I saw him put something in his pocket, at each of the wagons, but it was too dark for me to tell what it was," said Dan.

"Alright, Coyote and I will give those wagons a once over. Maybe it is something we can determine, before we set out today. If not, we will have to wait until something happens. I don't want to do that, but we may have no choice," said Sasa.

After her breakfast, Sasa took Coyote aside and told him what Dan had said. They began to look at the three wagons, one by one, searching the side of the wagon, that faced the fire, the night before. But, they could not find anything wrong. Everything looked in place. They had no choice, but to let the three wagons fall in line with the rest, as the train pulled out of camp.

*****

Capt. Evans had sent out the scouts, to make sure of the water and grass up ahead. The scouts came back and said there were scanty grass and water. An argument erupted among the various wagon owners. Some wanted to divide the company, some going due north. So Capt. Evans decided that he would take the company north for one day and then decide which way to go.

The train set out in the early morning. For the most part the way stayed fairly flat, with rolling hills off in the distance. Peter Diggin's wagon, stayed in line with the others, when suddenly, his wheel hit a medium sized rock. The wheel began to wobble loose on the axle. Peter could feel the wagon sway, but he was unaware of the problem causing it. Finally, the wheel slipped off and the wagon listed dangerously. Peter brought the wagon to a quick stop, causing all the wagons behind him to stop as well. Peter was surveying the damage, when Coyote rode up.

"Well, this must be what you were looking for this morning, Coyote," said Peter.

"We were just checking. We had no idea this was going to happen. Have you determined what caused the wheel to come off?" asked Coyote.

"Yes, the linchpin is gone. I don't know if it came off on the trail, but it is gone all the same. I have another, but I will need help, getting the wagon level, to slip the wheel back on. It's going to delay the train a bit, but with help, it will go quicker," said Peter.

Coyote realized, he would have to check all three of the wagons they had searched that morning, with no delay. Chances were, their linchpins were missing as well. When he checked, he found he was correct. He did not explain anything to the owners of the wagons, only that they were missing their linchpins and needed to replace them before the train set off again. Thank goodness, they caught the problem, before all the other wheels fell off.

Once Peter's wagon was repaired and the linchpins replaced, on all three wagons, the train was able to continue on. Nothing was said to Henley, even though Coyote knew, he was the one who sabotaged the wagons. Coyote was not ready to risk the peace of the train, let alone Dan's wish to remain anonymous. Now, they would have to keep a closer eye on Henley's movements. For that, he would need to use Wheezer and Yellow Eyes.

Sickness was beginning to plague the train, since they crossed the North Platte River. Mountain men called the illness, Mountain Fever, and it was a common ailment, in that area of the Rocky Mountains. Some of the ill were, J.M. Mathews, Porter Pyeatt, Andrew Pyeatt, John Kellum, James Carnahan and John Carnahan. Of the Cherokees the ill were, O.W. Lipe, Daniel Gunter and Martin Schrimsher. Others would follow, and thankfully, they all would recover.

Capt. Evans determined, that he would go due west through the Great Divide Basin and the Red Desert. The ones that wanted to keep going north, changed their minds and stuck with Capt. Evans, keeping the entire train together. The travelers did not realize, when it was, that they actually crossed the Great Divide. Game was more plentiful, than they had experienced on the entire trip.

Buffalo, elk, deer, bear, antelope and smaller game were available to the most inexperienced of hunters.

But soon, things turned quickly serious, when they were forced to camp beside a salt lake. By morning three oxen were dead and the rest of the animals were sick, from drinking the water of the lake. The next camp was a dry camp and they were forced to use the water in their kegs. It would take many days for the animals to recover from drinking the salt water.

The train traveled three more days and at each camp, there was no grass or water, for man or beast. Things were becoming desperate, when Capt. Evans sent out all men who owned horses, to look for water. However, some of the men went on foot. It was one of these men, who came back to camp, with a report, of a small pond of water from a heavy rain. That is what saved them, for it would be until the next camp, a hard day's journey, that they would find any water at all.

Finally, on July 25th, they crossed a branch of the Green River, which gave them plenty of water to fill their barrels and water their stock. On July 30th, Capt. Evans was forced to turn the company north, because the route west was impassable by wagons. The country was sandy and desolate. They camped that night, and the next, in a area with abundant grass, which gave them a little time for their stock to recoup.

Finally, they reached the main channel of the Green River. For several days, they traveled along, parallel to the Green River. Then Capt. Evans turned the company due west, again away from the river, but eventually they would cross the Green River again.

Chapter 21

Coyote had had enough of Henley Hughes. He knew, Henley was responsible for the removing of the linchpins, from the Cherokee's wagons. Who knew, what the man would try next. However, Coyote was not one to go telling tales to the wagon master. He would try to take care of this himself. He hoped that Henley would listen to reason, but something had to be done, because the sabotaging could become deadly, in rougher country. Sasa was not so sure it was a good idea to confront him. She saw Henley as an unbalanced man, who hated Indians and would stop at nothing to achieve his goal. Confronting him, could be dangerous.

Wheezer had been vigilant at watching the wagons overnight and so far Henley had not tried anything again, in the last few days. He saw Henley walk his oxen out of camp to picket them on the sparse grass and then saw Coyote follow. Wheezer decided he might be needed and followed behind Coyote. Coyote stopped in front of Henley, so Wheezer settled in a clump of grass, where Henley could not see him.

Coyote approached Henley with nothing in his hands, but Henley reacted as if Coyote carried a weapon.

"What do you want? I don't have any business with the likes of you. If'n you want someone to talk to, go to your own kind, but get away from me," said Henley.

"I just wanted to ask you why, you are sabotaging the Cherokee wagons? We know it was you, because you were seen. I'm coming to you, but I can go to Capt. Evans instead, if that's what you want," said Coyote.

"You filthy Indian, you have no right to question a good American like me. You get away from me now or I will break your neck," yelled Henley.

"Capt. Evans it is," said Coyote, as he turned to leave.

Henley knew he might be thrown off of the train, if the wagon master found out what he had been doing, so he lunged at Coyote's retreating form, grabbing hold of his shoulders. They fell to the ground, rolling in the sand and grass, kicking up dust into the still air. Henley pulled a sharp knife and straddled Coyote, sitting on his torso, his knife at Coyote's throat.

"I have had all I can stand of you Indians. I'm going to rid this train of you, once and for all!" said Henley.

When Henley raised his arm, to bring the knife down into Coyote's chest, Wheezer lunged and seized Henley's arm. The thrust, from Wheezer's body, knocked Henley off of Coyote and he quickly got up. Henley thrashed around, with Wheezer hanging on, until Coyote called Wheezer off. By that time, others had gathered around the fighting, wondering what had caused it. Some of them had been shouting, for Henley to kill the Indian. The Cherokees took note, of the volatile nature of the crowd.

Henley sat on the ground, his arm and wrist bleeding, but seemed not to notice the onlookers. Finally, Capt. Evans appeared.

"What on God's good earth is going on here?" roared Capt. Evans.

"Do you want to tell him, or should I?" said Coyote to Henley.

Henley sat where he was, at a loss for what to say. Soon Sasa came forward and spoke to Capt. Evans.

"Captain, we have been suffering sabotage, of the Cherokee wagons, for weeks now. It started with, someone putting salt peter in our drinking water. The second time, the culprit was seen. Henley Hughes removed the linchpins from our wheels, a few nights ago. That was what caused our delay, the other morning. I suspect, if you search his wagon, you will find the linchpins he removed, unless he threw them away. Regardless, someone saw him, and he does not deny it," said Sasa.

"Is this true Henley? Have you been causing these people trouble on the train?" said Capt. Evans.

But, Henley refused to answer at all. He just sat there, grumbling to himself. No one came to his defense.

"Well then, I will have to think on this, before I decide what to do. Until then Henley, your wagon will be up front in the train, where I can keep an eye on you. At night, I will not tolerate you wandering around, so I give permission for anyone seeing you near the Indians wagons, to knock you down and hogtie you," said Capt. Evans.

Henley rose from the ground, dusted himself off and went to his wagon. Capt. Evans had given the order, to move Henley's wagon, so that it would be at the front of the train in the morning. The onlookers dispersed, some shaking their heads. The Cherokees were still upset, though. There had been a lot of racial unrest on the train and they did not think Henley was the only one who wished them ill. It was hard to travel, day after day, with people that made no secret of their dislike for you.

Sasa wondered why those people agreed to come on this trip. They knew they would be traveling with the Cherokees, so why complain now? Something else had occurred to her. Could Henley be the one who murdered Albert Langley? Was that the beginning of his rampage? She might pose these questions to Coyote. Maybe he could help sort it out.

But the sentiment against the Cherokees worried Sasa even more. This might become a desperate situation. Given the mood of the Cherokees as well, Sasa was afraid the struggle between the two factions would result in a bloodbath. She could not let it come to that. She had to find a way to stop it from exploding.

Sasa went back to her wagon; it would soon be time to fix the evening meal. Coyote met her at the back of their wagon, while Stan was finishing picketing the stock.

"Well, that did not go well, did it?" said Coyote.

"It could have been worse. He could have killed you, and I would not want that. I love you too much to lose you now. But, I am worried. Did you hear the shouts against the Cherokees and Indians, in general, during the fight?" said Sasa.

"Yes I did, but I could not pay much attention to it at that moment. I was kind of busy. I do know, that the division between whites and Indians, on this train, is getting wider. I think a split is bound to happen, and soon," said Coyote.

"That frightens me, Coyote. We have traveled this far without bloodshed. I hate to think, it will come to that," said Sasa.

"It will have to happen sometime. It is inevitable, that eventually the whites will turn on the Indians. So do not be surprised, when it happens," said Coyote.

"I was also hoping, we would figure out who killed Albert. Do you think it was Henley? He hates Indians enough. I would not put it past him," said Sasa.

Coyote thought for a moment, before answering. He pulled out the chain and cross, from his medicine bag around his neck, and showed it to her.

"I found this, next to Albert's body. I have been keeping it, and trying to figure out, who it would have come from. Peter Diggins says, he never saw it before, and didn't think it belonged to Albert. So, that means, that it was probably ripped off of the killer, during the struggle in the wagon, when Albert was killed. Henley is not a religious person, so I doubt it is his," said Coyote.

"Why have you not told me this before?" said Sasa.

"I was not sure it belonged to the killer. But I think, I have come to the conclusion, that it must have," said Coyote.

Stan came around the corner of the wagon and noticed Coyote and Sasa talking.

"Is everything alright? What have you got there?" said Stan.

"Well, this was found by Albert's body. We are trying to figure out, who it belongs to," said Coyote.

Stan took the chain and cross, and examined them closely. Something about the necklace stirred a memory in him, but he did not dare say anything yet. He had to have time to think. He handed it back to Coyote.

"It looks familiar, but let me think on it a while. It may come to me, if'n I can just remember," said Stan.

Coyote nodded and slipped the necklace back into the pouch. As he turned to unpack part of his mess kit for dinner, Capt. Evans came around the corner of the wagon.

"Coyote, may I have a word with you?" said Capt. Evans.

"Yes, may Sasa join us?" asked Coyote.

"I guess she can hear, what I have to say," said Capt. Evans.

The three of them, and Wheezer, walked out away from the wagons and stopped by a small tree.

"Coyote, I am becoming increasingly worried about the mood of the train. This thing with Henley is just the tip, of the mountain of hate that is building up against the Cherokee. I am afraid that I won't be able to contain it, if another fight breaks out," said Capt. Evans.

"What do you want me to do, Captain? It does not seem to matter, that the Cherokees have done nothing wrong. It seems the closer we get to the gold, the worse it gets. I agree that Henley is not the only one causing the trouble," said Coyote.

"We are going to be pulling into Fort Bridger, probably tomorrow. I think we need to make some plans while we are there. I want to keep the company together. We still have a desert to cross and I don't need any troublemakers causing problems. We will have enough to deal with," said Capt. Evans.

"Alright, I will meet with you tomorrow night, we can talk then," said Coyote.

Sasa had remained quiet through the conversation, while Wheezer stayed at her side.

Chapter 22

Stan Grant had searched his memory concerning the chain and cross left at the scene of the murder of Albert Langley. He had a glimmer of recollection of one like it, hanging around the neck of someone he knew, but he could not imagine, that it had anything to do with that person. The person he was thinking of was back in Arkansas, going from homestead to homestead, comforting his flock of parishioners. It could not possibly be the same man.

The only thing he could do, now, was to get a better look at the face of the man, who claimed his wagon as his own. And there would be no better time, than while they were laying over at Fort Bridger. Instead of hiding, Stan was going to have to be bold, walk right up to the man and talk to him, face to face. So, he decided to take Coyote with him. Then they would find out once and for all, the identity of the man who stole his wagon and left him for dead on the road.

The next day, they traveled another fourteen miles, reaching Fort Bridger late in the afternoon.

Fort Bridger, by this time had been established as a trading post for several years, by James (Jim) Bridger and Louis Vasquez. On this day, Jim Bridger was welcoming them to the fort. There was a supply shop within the walls of the fort, which held all sorts of things, needed on the trail, but it also sold, one commodity, that caused much trouble among the Indians. Whiskey! For one dollar, the travelers could buy a bottle, and it was their first access to spirits, since they left home. Many of the travelers bought it, including some of the Cherokee, and were happily imbibing.

That night, the revelers got loud and boisterous, which rankled the nerves of those who did not drink alcohol. It was a recipe for disaster, if there ever was one. Capt. Evans stayed with the group of drinkers, trying to keep them contained and quiet, to no avail. He finally gave up and went back to camp.

This was the night that Stan decided to confront the man with his wagon. Coyote had not bought any of the whiskey and agreed to come with him. They walked around the circle of the wagon train, until finally they approached the man's wagon. It seemed he was inside, so Stan knocked on the back wooden gate. The man emerged from the wagon, with his hat pulled low.

"What do you want?" asked the man.

"We would like to talk to you, sir," said Stan.

"I am too busy! Come see me another day," said the man.

The man was now on his guard. This was what he had been afraid would happen, but he saw no way of avoiding the confrontation, now that Stan Grant was standing in front of him.

"I think not! Sir, this wagon does not belong to you. I am the rightful owner of it. Whoever stole this wagon from me left me to die along the road. I want to know who you are?" said Stan.

At that moment, Capt. Evans walked up.

"I heard what you said Stan. Is this true? This is your wagon? How do you know it is yours?" said Capt. Evans.

"I can prove it. I know where everything is and I have my name written on every tool inside it," said Stan.

"Then I reckon you best show me," said Capt. Evans.

At that, Stan jumped up into the wagon, walked past the man and picked up several items. He brought them out to Capt. Evans.

"You are absolutely right. These are your tools. What do you have to say for yourself, sir?" asked Capt. Evans.

The man jumped down from the wagon, without a word, and just stood there, not knowing what to do. Suddenly, Stan grabbed hold of the man's hat and yanked it off his head. When he did, Stan gasped, finally recognizing the man.

"Reverend, Phineas Piney? I don't believe it. He is the reverend that used to come to my home. He even tried to talk me out of going to California. Why? Why would you try to kill me? You could have asked to go with me. I might have let you come, but you did not have to shoot me and steal my wagon," said Stan.

The man stayed silent.

"I think that stealing this wagon is not all this man has done, Capt. Evans," said Coyote.

Coyote pulled the chain and cross out of his pouch and held it high for the captain to see.

"This was found next to Albert, the day we found his body. I could not figure who it belonged to, because Peter,

Albert's partner, had never seen it before. Now I see how it fits in. Captain, this is the murderer of Albert," said Coyote.

Finally, the Rev. Piney raised his head to speak.

"You think you are so clever. You are nothing, but a heathen Indian. I had every reason to silence that man. He recognized me and I knew he would ruin my trip to the gold," said Rev. Piney.

"How could he have recognized you? He was Cherokee, he didn't even live in Arkansas," asked Capt. Evans.

"We met, when Albert went to Fayetteville for supplies, he could not get into Fort Smith. I counselled him on the wages of drinking whiskey. He was drunk, at the time. Somehow, though, he remembered me. But I have every right to that gold, as much right and more than you Indians do," said Rev. Piney.

Capt. Evans shook his head. It was obvious that this Rev. Piney was off in his head. But what could he do about it? There was no law of the land here and he was not a sheriff. Some of the men in the train were shouting and wanting to hang Piney, but Evans did not feel he could let them do it. Chances were that if he just sent him away, alone on the prairie he would die anyway.

"Reverend Piney, I hereby banish you from this train. You are to leave this wagon, to its rightful owner, and be gone from here by morning. If you are not, I will allow the rest of the train, to take you in hand and meet out justice, in whatever way they see fit," said Capt. Evans.

Rev. Piney became enraged, at them, and pulled up his fists as if to strike.

"You will not stop me, from getting my share of the gold. You are a bunch of puny cowards, and you will see me again. I swear, you will curse this day," said Rev. Piney.

Stan took charge of his wagon. If Piney needed supplies, he could get them from the sutler, at the fort.

The revelers grew ever louder and tempers began to flare. By morning, there was a large group of travelers ready to fight. Capt. Evans had to find a way to defuse the anger, but the group was adamant.

"It's those darn Cherokees, just a bunch of drunken Indians. We don't need them on this train," said one traveler.

"We shoulda never agreed for them to come with us. They've been nothin' but trouble. Bet, we coulda been here long afore this, if they hadn't been on the train," said another traveler.

"Filthy Indians, don't have no right to that gold, anyhow. It's only for Americans. It's time we kicked their butts to the side of the road," said the next traveler.

Wheezer and Yellow Eyes stood away from the group, but Wheezer began to growl, at the sound of violence in their voices.

That was the general sentiment, of the gathering group of whites on the train. The Cherokees were just waking from their night of revelry and were wondering what the commotion was.

Capt. Evans approached Sasa and Coyote.

"I'm sorry about this, but it seems we have come to a division of the company. Do you have any suggestions on what to do?" said Capt. Evans.

"We are now on the California Road, which is plain on the maps, and Jim Bridger told Coyote, about the Hastings Cutoff. I think we can find our own way, from here. I vote, we separate our Cherokee wagons from the company. If any of the other wagons wish to join us, we do not mind. We will leave in the morning," said Sasa.

The Cherokees standing around, nodded their agreement, and went back to their wagons.

"I am afraid that I will have to go with the Cherokees, Capt. Evans. I will now scout for them," said Coyote.

"I hate to lose you, Coyote. But, I think it is for the best. Maybe we will see you in California, but it is a mighty big place. If not, then go with God," said Capt. Evans.

The angry group dispersed, satisfied that they would be better off without the Cherokees. Little did they realize, that it was the Cherokees blazing of the new trail, that had gotten them this far, without one single death from cholera. The same could not be said of the other routes, which claimed the lives of hundreds of people.

Chapter 23

Jim Bridger was up and ready to help the Cherokees on their way. He felt an affinity for them, since he had dealt with Indians, of all tribes, for many years. He would give them all the help he could.

Coyote and Sasa came into the sutler's shop, to finalize their purchases, when Jim Bridger walked in.

"Looks like you're about ready, I reckon. I forgot to mention, that your Cherokee brothers that left you at Pueblo, the ones who decided to pack, were through here on the 24th of this month. They left a message for you'all. They wanted you to know, that they came through, and they hoped to see you at the diggings in California," said Jim.

Sasa was elated to hear this. They had heard nothing of that group of packers, since they separated from the train and it was wonderful to hear.

"You keep in mind, the instructions I gave you about the Hensley Cutoff, which you will cross over and then the Hastings Cutoff, which you will take after Hastings Pass. You will be going through some very dry and hot desert. Just be sure, you're well rested and your stock is well watered, afore you attempt to cross," said Jim.

Coyote took careful note, of the instructions Jim gave, and soon they were on their way. The Cherokees were joined by a few white wagons, including Stan Grant and his newly regained wagon. There were twelve wagons in all, setting off on their own, into the unknown. However, their load was a bit lighter, knowing that they were leaving behind all the strife and hate, with the other group.

*****

Rev. Phineas Piney watched them go, from behind the trees, along the river, not too far off from Fort Bridger. He had no intention of losing sight of these wagons. He had an agenda to fulfill. He wanted his share of revenge and his plans included, killing as many of the Cherokees, as he could, as well as Stan Grant.

He had purchased supplies and a mule to carry them. He walked alongside it, as he followed the small wagon train of Cherokees. He paid no mind to the danger of crossing a desert, which had, already cost the lives of people and animals alike. But, he was not thinking of that.

Phineas was remembering all the years he struggled to tend a flock of parishioners, who paid him no mind. The farmers and families that he attended to, were apathetic and blind to his counsel. They listened to his sermons, then went right home and did what they wanted to. He was unappreciated and unrecognized, as an authority on God's word. He had gotten tired of preaching the gospel to them.

Then gold was found in California and half of his flock, was preparing to leave, to find their fortunes. He had struggled, with the pennies they gave to him to live on. It was time for him to find his own fortune and forget preaching, to undeserving peons. There was gold in California and it called to him. He felt it was his payment, from God, for all his hard work. But, too many people were getting in his way and he would not allow them to stop him. Stan Grant and his Indian friends would pay, for getting him kicked off the train. And so, he followed at a distance, never allowing them to know, he was just behind them, on the California Trail.

*****

Coyote led the way west from Fort Bridger. The days were hot and dry. So hot, that it made the skin sting and sweat to evaporate immediately. Soon, the wagons rolled into an area that had been inhabited by the Anasazi, in ancient times. It contained large sandstone spires that looked like needles, from far away. From there, they continued on through a huge canyon country, which took them many days to traverse. They finally reached the Weber River, where they stopped to recoup their animals and fill their water barrels.

A little more than a day's travel, took them to the new Salt Lake City, which was only about two years old now. The city was founded by Brigham Young, a religious man, who was also a politician and settler, which led a large group of followers. The group was known as Mormons and they had been chased out of several states. Finally, Brigham led the group to this desolate landscape, to try to make a place for them to live in peace. Already there were established farms, crops and shops, with building going on everywhere.

The crops were watered by an intricate system of irrigation, from the nearby springs. It seemed that the desert had blossomed. The travelers were kindly welcomed and were treated to freshly picked vegetables and fruit. They were astonished, to be eating watermelons and fresh corn. They also were taken by the kindness and gentleness of the people. It was hard to believe, that the Mormons were always at odds, with the United States and the Army.

It was already late in the summer, so they did not stay and pushed on after only two days of rest. Coyote scouted and then returned to the train, to lead them onward. In all their travels, up to now, they had not seen any Indians, hostile or otherwise, except for the Osage, back in Indian Territory. However, they were beginning to see skeletal remains of dead oxen and graves along the road, at almost every mile. Those were the cholera victims, who had come using the Independence, Missouri route that was called the Santa Fe Trail or the Oregon Trail, further north. Seeing all the death along the way, made them appreciate what they had successfully done. They had blazed a new trail to Santa Fe and then a new trail to Fort Bridger. It had kept them from the same illnesses, that plagued the immigrants, in which had come on other routes.

The route they were now on, was being called the Mormon Trail and there were markers along the way. However, they were not needed. So many people and wagons had traveled on this road, already, that the trail was plain to see. Soon, they would be coming to the Hastings Cutoff, which began at the Hastings Pass. It was miles of treacherous desert, but would take them to Huntington's Creek and then Mary's River. The travelers began to notice, more and more furniture being discarded along the way, to lighten the load for sick and dying oxen. So far, they had not had to do this. Only time would tell, if they too, would need to discard items, to cross the desert.

They were heading for the desert and the air was already so hot, it was hard to breath. Dan had been drinking water, but she never seemed to get enough. A coating of salt dusted her skin and her lips were beginning to crack. She was unaware of Peter Diggins, watching her from the wagon, just behind hers. She was feeling a little faint, but she kept on going.

As her wagon rolled along, behind another, she thought about the split from the main wagon train. She actually felt safer in some ways, because she was surrounded by other Cherokees, with only a few whites in the small train. However, in some ways, it caused problems for her. It made it harder for her to keep her identity a secret, with so few in their party and that fact worried her. She was not sure, what the other Cherokees would think, about a woman alone on their wagon train. So she kept her secret.

Soon, the heat overcame her and she slumped down on the seat and passed out. Her oxen continued on for a time, but then slowed to a stop. Peter stopped his wagon behind hers, jumped down from his and mounted the back of hers. He made his way past the boxes and bags to reach her on the front seat. She was mumbling to herself, but totally limp. Peter pulled her into the covered part of the wagon and quickly found the canteen by his side. He poured some water on his handkerchief and put the cool compress on her forehead and cheeks.

Her hat had fallen off to reveal a smooth forehead. He stroked her hair for a moment or two, then left her there while he went to fetch Coyote. He knew that Coyote was trained as a Medicine Man and knew the healing arts. By that time, the front of the train had stopped, while Coyote went to investigate.

Sasa showed up at the back of the wagon, at about the same time as Coyote. Sasa had not said anything to Coyote about Dan's identity, but if Coyote was going to treat her, he would need to know.

"Coyote, before you go to help, I need to tell you something. Dan is not who you think," she whispered.

"Don't worry Sasa. I figured it out a long time ago. I know that Dan is woman. Her secret is safe," said Coyote.

He hopped up into Dan's wagon and began to try to bring her around. He took out of his herbal pack, a small bag of mineral salts. He poured into his had a small amount, and to that, he added a drop or two of oil of peppermint. He held this under Dan's nose and slowly she became aware of her surroundings. He then rubbed a drop of the peppermint oil on each wrist and began fanning her. Soon she was fully awake and wondering what had happened.

"What's going on? What happened? I was driving my team and then everything went black," said Dan.

"You fainted from the heat. You will be fine, but you need to drink more water," said Coyote.

"I have been, but I can't quench my thirst," said Dan.

"I am going to make camp here, until the sun starts going down. Then tonight, we will continue on, when it is cooler. We won't make camp until late. Meanwhile, you need to rest and drink as much as you can. If you don't, your kidneys could shut down and that would be very bad. Also, you are wearing too many clothes," said Coyote.

The comment startled Dan. She had been wearing extra clothes, to conceal her body shape. Coyote saw the look of confusion on her face and decided to address it.

"Dan, I am already aware, that you are a woman. You should be wearing light cotton, not heavy flannel, like you have on now. I will not tell anyone, but if you want to stay alive, you are going to have to change into something cooler. In fact, I don't think anyone on this train, will care one way or another, if you are woman or man. I would consider letting them know," said Coyote.

"No! If everyone knew, then I may not be able to stake a claim for the gold," said Dan.

"No, but you won't stake a claim if you are dead, either," said Coyote.

That brought Dan up short. She knew that Coyote was only speaking sense, but she was so afraid that this trip will have been for nothing. She would have to decide, and soon. Peter showed up at the back of the wagon. Coyote left to organize the brief campsite and Peter jumped up into the wagon.

"How are you feeling now?" asked Peter.

"Silly," said Dan.

"Nothing silly about it, heat can get to anyone. I overheard what Coyote told you about the clothes. But, I wanted to tell you something important," said Peter.

Now Dan was anxious. What could this man want to say to her?

"What?" she answered.

"First, I want you to know, that I have no ulterior motive in telling you this. I just want to help and be your friend," said Peter.

Dan stayed quiet, almost holding her breath.

"I know that you are a woman, but it does not matter to me. I will keep your secret, if you want, or I will stand by you if the rest of the train finds out. I will not let anyone hurt you," said Peter.

Dan was astonished. She had not seen this coming and she had no idea that Peter knew. Now, it seemed that her secret was leaking out and soon the entire small wagon train would know. Now, she would need to think hard about revealing it to the rest of the train. There were other women on the train, not just Sasa. But, they were accompanying their husbands. She was still, a woman alone. It would help to have a friend that is a man.

"I accept your friendship, Peter. But, I will have to think, if I am going to tell the rest of the train or not. I want to stake a claim for the gold and I am afraid that they won't let a woman, alone, work a claim," said Dan.

"If that is your worry, then let me try to think of a solution as well. Two minds are better than one, so don't agonize over it," said Peter.

She placed her hat back on her head and slipped out of the wagon, to start to make camp. There was only sparse grass here. Probably, the only grass they would see until after they crossed the desert. So after picketing her oxen, she began scything up as much of the grass as she could. Peter worked too and they piled the grass in the back of each of their wagons. Peter made sure Dan drank sufficient water and reminded her to choose some cooler clothes.

*****

Rev. Piney had followed a closely as he dared. He had hoped that he would overtake them, before they entered the desert, but it seemed they were planning on traveling at night. He was tired and hot, and he was ready to rest. He thought, *they can't get too far ahead in just one night. I can catch up to them by tomorrow, if'n I start early. And when I do, I can figure out a way to sabotage their wagons and they can die in the desert.*

He was satisfied with his thoughts; however, he was not paying much attention to his own physical needs. His boots had already worn holes in the soles and were coming apart at the seams. He passed clumps of grass, but did not stop to allow his mule to feed on them. He only drank a small amount of water at any time. His mind was on other things, he thought more important.

He paid little mind to his cracking lips or the salt dust covering his clothes. He was totally consumed with the idea of finding ways to make the Cherokee wagon train pay, for causing him to be kicked off the Evans/Cherokee train. Plus, Stan Grant was one of the whites that were with the Cherokees and he still wanted to confiscate his wagon yet again, leaving Stan dead in the desert.

So Phineas stopped, made camp and rested through the night. The next day, he could no longer see the Cherokees in the distance, but their trail was plain to see. He began walking and paid no attention to the wagons and items left to rot in the desert. His mule shied away from the smell of death, coming from the dead oxen that lay, on either side of the trail. It did not occur to him, that he might find needed items or tools in the abandoned goods.

His mind was on one thing and one thing only. Revenge!

Chapter 24

Willie Catcher watched, as the camp began to pack up, for another evening of travel. It seemed a much easier way to traverse the desert and everyone's spirits were high. He still missed his wife terribly, but the closer they came to California, the more excited he got about the gold. He was comfortable with the small train. It was a relief to travel in peace.

The night, before they stopped at a well-worn campsite to make camp, until the latter part of the next day, a party of Shoshones approached and turned out to be a friendly sort of tribe. It was remarked, that they were a very handsome people and they spoke with the universal sign language, in which, they all knew. The white members of the train, were astonished that there had been no hostilities, and were delighted, that they had chosen to come with the Cherokees.

Willie was pleased to have met the Shoshones, because they had given them some very good advice, about crossing the desert and finding the Mary River. The Shoshones knew all of the springs that could be had, in the desert, and would make their crossing much safer.

At each campsite, Willie took the time to write in his journal, about the previous days travel. Then, when he wrote to his wife, he would have all the information he needed to help her to see his journey, the way he was seeing it. He wrote to her regularly, but could only send the letters at stops, where there were people traveling, the other direction. When these travelers made it to Independence, Missouri, they would send his letters. It would take months for her to get them, but he knew, that she would rather have that, than no letters at all.

Once he was in California, he would have better opportunities to send letters, but the letters would probably have to be sent by boat and still take months to get to Indian Territory. He loved his wife so much, he wanted to make sure she did not forget him or presume him dead. He would head home, as soon as he could.

*****

They were making more miles at night, than they had been, when traveling during the day. The only disadvantage was trying to sleep, in the heat of the day. They could imagine, what it would be like to travel during the day, and they were thankful that they were not trying to cross in the heat.

They continued to see abandoned wagons and a few wagons sunk down in what used to be mud. It must have rained and turned the desert into mire. Once the wheels sink in, there was nothing to be done, but leave the wagon behind. The ground was hard and dry now. Seeing this made them hope, there would not be rain, while they were still in the desert.

They would be going through the Hastings Pass today and then on through the Hastings Cutoff. There had been warnings about taking this route, but it also cut many miles off of their trip, if they took it. A previous wagon train had taken this route in 1846. They were the Donner/Reed party. They took too long to make it across the cutoff and wound up, trapped by snow in the mountains. Everyone knew the story and there were rumors of cannibalism, associated with it.

But the small Cherokee train, would be coming through the cutoff, much earlier than the Donner party had, so this knowledge gave them courage to take that route. After going through the pass, they found sparse grass and dry dusty ground. No water was yet, anywhere to be found. They traveled by day and by night, only allowing short periods of rest. They came upon the mud flats, which showed a complicated pattern of cracks in the crust of the desert. Under the dried mud, was soft silt, in which, wagons and animals could sink into, if the drivers were not very careful.

Continuing on each day and night, the party kept their sites on a mountain top, called Pilot Peak. At the base of that mountain would be a spring, which was, the first water for their animals, in over ninety miles of dry merciless desert. The oxen suffered, but most kept going dutifully. A few became crazed, broke free and ran off to probably to die. The travelers could see great swaths of water, which turned out to be a mirage. So, it made it difficult to tell, what was real and what was not.

Finally, the wagons rolled up to the springs, at the bottom of Pilot Peak. They could not take the time to rest for very long, for they dare not be caught in the mountains when the snows came, like the Donners had done.

Then, they went around the south end of the Ruby Mountains and drove north, where they struck a stream called Huntington's Creek. The water was a bit brackish, but it was a welcome sight. They continued going north until they struck Mary's River, which turned them west towards Emigrant Pass.

It was now late September and the nights were getting uncomfortably cold. They were able to make fourteen, to twenty miles, each day. They had weathered the worst of the desert and now had to contend with rugged mountainous country. They were all tired and worn, but they knew their goal was close, so they pressed on.

*****

Nothing was going to stop Phineas Piney, but on days like today, he was tempted to quit. He was exhausted, sick and hurting. He had fallen several times, causing many cuts and abrasions on his skin. The salt from the desert, coated his wounds, making them sting. His left arm was now tied up in a sling, with a possible break. His mule was limping and he had to whip it, to force it to continue on, but it was not going to last much longer.

He had pushed so hard to catch up with the wagon train, that he had left part of his supplies, at one of his camps. He was now out of flour, coffee and low on water. In fact, he had stopped giving water to his mule. But today, he finally struck Huntington Creek. There were parties of wagons behind him, almost overtaking him. But he could not allow that to happen. Hundreds of people were on the trail to find gold in California. The fewer people that saw him, the better. He pressed on and on. He even walked through the night and the day, in order to catch up. He could tell he was getting closer to finding the Cherokees, because he found their last campsite and their fire pits were still warm. But, he was no closer to figuring out how to accomplish his revenge.

When he struck Mary's River, his mule began to perk up some, but she still limped badly. He could not afford to stop and that meant that he would have to leave her behind soon. He would have to carry his supplies on his own back, but he would go as fast as his own legs could carry him. He was determined to catch up to them, whatever the cost.

*****

Dan had lain awake for several hours the night, before trying to decide what to do. She knew it was only a matter of time, before someone else on the train realized the truth. Sasa and Peter had figured it out. What might happen to her if she was found out at the diggings and she was alone? She had no defense. Once she was exposed, she knew there were few options for her. She needed the protection of a man to make it work. Peter had offered to be her protector, but she was very unsure. He had been nothing but kind, since he revealed he knew her secret. He might be the answer.

Sasa, Wheezer, Coyote and Yellow Eyes sat in front of their campfire resting, after a long day of travel. The days were still hot, but not like the desert and they no longer had to travel at night. The other Cherokees were preparing for their evening meal and Sasa was going to have to get started on their meal soon. It was nice to have this time to relax and contemplate their journey.

The few whites on the train were getting along splendidly, with the Cherokees. Stan Grant, now in charge of his own wagon, was in good spirits, as were the other whites, which, had chosen to come with the Cherokees.

Most everyone had started their fires, around the circle, near the middle, which gave them plenty of light. Dan and Peter were now cooking together, which made it easier for both of them. But, Dan was still reserved and she looked as if something was bothering her. Unexpectedly, Dan came up to the campfire to speak with Sasa and Coyote.

"I think, I am ready, to tell the train my secret. I've been thinking about it and I decided that it was going to be hard to keep it a secret, at the gold fields. There will be little privacy there and I think I was deluding myself that I could do this alone. Peter and I have made a deal to work a claim together, sharing the profits. His being there, will give me a measure of security," said Dan.

With that quick proclamation Dan stepped to the center, where the light from the fires shone on her short cut black hair, and she began to speak.

"I have an announcement. Some of you may care and others may not, but I feel it is important for me to tell you, that I have been keeping a secret. My name is really Danica Mosely, not Dan. That is a woman's name and I am a woman. I am Wolf Clan. My husband died and I wanted to try for the gold in California, but I did not think I would be accepted, as a woman alone. I just want to say, that I am sorry for lying to you all. I will now partner with Peter at the diggings. That is all I have to say," said Danica.

There were looks of astonishment around the circle, but no frowns. All of a sudden, there started an applause, which built, until every member of the small wagon train was clapping in favor of Danica. She smiled her appreciation and with tears in her eyes, went back to her wagon.

*****

The Cherokee train was now following what was known as the California Trail, which ran along Mary's River and then the Humboldt River. Excitement was building. They knew that the Humboldt ended, at the Humboldt Sink, where the stream disappeared into the ground. But a discussion among them, suggested that they take a different route, one that would take them further north, just before they reached the sink. It was called the Applegate – Lassen Trail. Then once they crossed into California, they still had many miles to go, to make it to the diggings. But, it was just the thought that they were so close to California, which excited them all.

It was now the middle of October. They still had to get over the mountains, before they were snowed in. The small group of Cherokees and whites came to a place on the Humboldt River, where a beautiful meadow was marked as Lassen's Meadow. Here is where the road split. They could go south or they could go northwest on the Applegate – Lassen Trail. They chose the latter and hurried on.

Soon, they were entering a vast plain of greasewood shrubs, rough grasses and black rocks. This place was called the Black Rock Desert. It was advertised, that it stretched over one hundred miles, before they would strike the Feather River. But in reality, it ended up adding, over two hundred miles to their trip. The travelers were unwary, and they had no idea, that the Lassen Cutoff was going to be treacherous. It was pioneered by Peter Lassen, who had advertised his cutoff to benefit himself.

The black rocks were ancient lava flows. The region was only semi-arid, not a completely dry desert. They would find colorful rock canyons and a large playa of mud flats. There were springs here and there, along the way, and pools of sulfur infused water. There was enough good water to get them across, but there were many other problems in traversing this path. By the time the travelers realized their mistake, it was too late to turn back.

The main train they had split off from, had taken the southern route, called the Truckee Branch, but there was no time to backtrack and get over the mountains before the snows came. So, on they went, trying to follow a road that had proved fatal to others who took this trail. Two of the wagons had to be abandoned, because of crushed wheels from the rugged rocks that were impossible to miss.

Everyone on the train suffered, but continued to push on. It was vital they make it over the mountains. If not, then certain doom awaited them.

*****

As he stumbled along after the wagon train, Phineas began to think he might not make it. He fell regularly and the black lava rocks cut slices into his legs, arms and hands. They continually stung from the sweat that ran down his body. He drank often from his canteen, but the water stunk like sulfur and was almost unpalatable. It was all he had to quench his thirst. He figured that he was a day behind the train, but he was losing ground, because of his injuries. He had been forced to leave his mule behind and carried as much as he could, in a bag that he draped over his back.

His shoes were in shreds, but he had taken a bit of leather and wrapped them, so they would stay together. When he could, he stopped to hunt fresh meat. There were always rabbits or small rodents he could eat. He had kept his strike-a-lite to start a fire, when he needed one, but he did not want to bring attention to himself. His biggest concern was the local Indians. Whenever he needed a fire, he made sure to camp where hills and rocks surrounded him, which was not hard to do in this rough country.

There were fewer other travelers on this road, since most would take the southern route. But he still worried that those traveling behind him would catch up. He had no choice, but to push on as hard as he could. Every night, he wracked his brain to find ways to bring ruin to the people of the wagon train, and mostly to Stan Grant. But each day, he was getting weaker, with each step he took. His arm was still in a sling, which made it hard to hunt. The swelling had gone down, but he had no use of his arm and hand.

Every time he thought of quitting his pursuit for revenge, he talked himself out of it. He kept on remembering the people who paid no attention to his needs back home and he would not go back to that. After he accomplished his action against the train, he would still be able to make a claim to the gold. He was a driven man.

Chapter 25

Finally, the train made Lassen's Pass, passing by two lakes, one on either side of the trail. The group pressed on and soon came to Goose Lake. Here is where they encountered troops, heading in the opposite direction. The troops were carrying supplies for Fort Hall. They camped together that night and for the first time, the Cherokees got true mileage to the gold diggings. To their dismay, it was going to be another two hundred eighty seven miles, to the first, of the gold camps.

"The road gets longer every day," said one of the Cherokees.

"We have no choice but to continue. But at least now, we know exactly where we are headed and how far it is, given to us by the U.S. Army," said Coyote.

After the troop departed their camp, Coyote took Sasa and Stan aside for a private conference, behind the wagon.

"I had one of the scouts backtrack last night and I have some news, we may not be happy about," said Coyote.

"Why would you backtrack the way we have already come? Do you think Indians are following us?" said Sasa.

"No, not Indians, but someone is. A small night fire was spotted last night and the scout said, it was the fire of one lone man. He did not approach the camp, but came back to report. I have a sinking feeling, who it is, that would travel alone in Indian country. There are several trains behind us, but this man does not join up with them and travels alone. That can only mean that he does not want to be observed," said Coyote.

"I can't imagine what a feller would be doin' out alone," said Stan.

"Who do you think it is, Coyote?" said Sasa.

"Well, the other train could have kicked Henley off, but I don't see that he would travel by himself. I think it might be the Reverend Piney. So, we need to be on the watch. If it is Piney, then we may be in for some trouble," said Coyote.

"I don't care, no never mind, if'in it is Piney. He's gonna haveta work hard to do anythin' to us," said Stan.

"All the same, we need to be on our guard for when he catches up to us. In this mountain country, it could take him several days to gain on us, but we still need to keep it in mind," said Coyote.

Every night, the three made an effort to keep an eye out, for any trace of a campfire, and every day when they came to the top of a ridge, they looked back along their trail for the follower. But, it was several days before he was spotted, limping along the trail, in obvious pain and misery.

*****

They crossed over the north fork, of the Pit River, and from there, they followed the river south. They were still in the mountains, which meant, that they went up and down the ridges, as the trail took them, but they only made six or seven miles, as the crow flies. Then, the Pit River, took an abrupt turn west, but their instructions said, to follow the trail south, crossing Horse Creek and then striking the Susan River.

Just as they crossed the Susan River, it started to snow in earnest. Up until now, the snow was in spirts and starts, only amounting to a few inches, here and there. But, this time the sky looked like it was ready to drop several feet of snow onto their trail. They estimated, they had another sixty miles, to the first of the digging camps. These camps were located, after Lassen's Rancho, where Lassen evidently lived. They continued to get word from the scouts, that there was still a lone follower and behind him, many groups of travelers. It looked as if they were at the head of the migration and they wanted to stay in the lead.

Coyote advised them they push on from morning to dusk, giving them a few more hours of travel. Hopefully, the snow would not mound up, so high, that they could not make it through. It continued to snow throughout the night and the next morning, they would have to distinguish the trail, as best they could. Thank goodness for the scouts, for they blazed the trail in front of them.

* * * * *

Rev. Piney struggled against the falling snow. Step by step he carried on. He allowed his hate for the people traveling ahead of him, to push him on, but it was their tracks that told him where to step. Because of the snow, the wagons were going much slower and as long as he kept to the grooves the wagon wheels made, he could gain on them. He was sure that he would overtake the train by the time they reached the first digging camps, but what then? He had no idea, what to do next. However, he was sure, that an opportunity to land a blow, to the whole train, would appear. At the very least, he would get his revenge on Stan Grant, who should have stayed dead the first time.

He could no longer feel his arm in the sling. He tried to move his hand, but it was like the signal had been cut from his brain. The skin of his arm had turned black and mottled. One thing, the cold did for him, was that he no longer felt the sting of his cuts and abrasions. His shoes were long since gone and now, he walked with only rags covering his feet. He was totally out of provisions, but he still could catch, an unwary rabbit. However, there was no dry wood to be had, so, he was forced to eat the meat raw. He ate the snow for water and as long as he kept moving, he did not get over-chilled. He knew deep inside, that his quest was coming to an end soon. Then, he would be able to claim, his rightful share, of the abundance of gold that God had provided for him.

*****

Sasa was worried about Coyote. He spent long hours out in the cold, but never complained. He had told her that his people were used to the cold, but it was hard for her to imagine, since she was raised in a temperate climate. Wheezer stayed by her side, most of the day, but occasionally he ventured out. It looked as if he was checking the back trail, then he would return seemingly worried about something. Yellow Eyes stayed with Coyote and thrived in the cold and snow. But, Wheezer did not have the type of coat that could keep him warm, out in the weather, like Yellow Eyes had.

Wheezer had just returned from one of his forays along the back trail. He jumped up on the forward seat with Sasa

169

and put is head in her lap. She wished she could speak dog language, because she was sure, that he had something he wished to tell her. Instead, he seemed to be waiting for something to happen. That made Sasa nervous. She knew Wheezer's heart and if he was concerned about something, then she should be, also.

The snow was getting deep and several times the wagons had to be pushed from behind, to get them unstuck from ruts in the trail. Every member of the train was now on foot, guiding their footsore oxen on, while others pushed their wagons, from behind. They all had to work together, to get the whole train through. The time had come for them to lighten their loads, so they discarded as much of their items, as was not absolutely necessary, and pitched them to the side of the trail.

They finally came to a clearing, a few miles after crossing a near frozen Deer Creek. They pulled into a camp of other travelers. A man approached the lead wagon and announced his name as Mr. Bruff. He was encamped here, guarding the possessions of his company, who went on ahead. They would send a rescue party back for their goods and for Bruff. Meanwhile, he welcomed those who wandered into his camp.

That evening, Bruff told them of the difficulties that lie ahead, when they finally would come to the base of the Sierra Nevada Mountains. Sacramento lay on the other side, but the early snows would make it hard for them to get across. His advice was for them, to discard even more of their possessions, to lighten the loads on their oxen. It could mean life or death. After a meager meal, the travelers gleaned through their belongings again, to see what they could get rid of, that they did not need to sustain life.

Later that evening, another company of travelers pulled into camp, very tired and footsore. But, with the snow still falling and their concentration focused on their chores, the Cherokees did not have an opportunity to meet any of them. They missed seeing Rev. Phineas Piney slip into camp. He had taken advantage of the discarded items the Cherokees had left behind, a few miles back, finding a pair of worn shoes among the items they had thrown out. That find alone had helped him immensely.

The next evening, they found themselves at the base of the Sierra Nevada Mountains, so they camped and readied themselves for the last push. The snow had slacked off and the next day dawned bright and sunny, yet very cold. They started up the trail, which was slow going indeed. They had given their oxen extra hay, to help them with the energy they would need, but the oxen were in poor condition already.

However, the scenery was spectacular. The tall pines that covered the hills, and the rocks, covered with snow, resembled a fairyland one might read about in a book. The sun glinted off of the snow in the trees and everything sparkled.

But, the travelers did not have time to enjoy the view. Their trail was increasingly difficult. The danger was that they would be caught in the mountains when a snow storm happened, which could bury them, like it had, the Donner party.

The travelers were not exactly alone anymore. Other parties were coming up behind. When they camped for the night, they could mingle a bit and get to know their fellow travelers. Unfortunately, some of the other travelers were wary of the Cherokee, not knowing, that they were as civilized as themselves.

* * * * *

Phineas had camped with the company that was just behind the Cherokee party. That gave him easy access to the wagons ahead. He had shared a fire, with a group of men from Missouri. He sat by the fire, even after they all went to bed, tired from their day of difficult travel.

When he found himself totally alone, he took a tin cup and filled it with glowing coals from the fire and started for the Cherokee camp. It was not hard to find the wagon that belonged to Stan Grant. Stan was asleep inside, so he had to be very quiet and careful. He crept up to the back of the wagon, lifted the back covering sheet and emptied the cupful of coals on the floor. It might take several minutes for a fire to start, but by that time, he would be safely, back in the other camp.

*****

Wheezer was restless that night. He kept hearing noises that made him stay awake and alert. Finally, he got up and decided to patrol the wagons, once again. Yellow Eyes was off hunting in the dark, so Wheezer would patrol alone. His padded feet, walked quietly, on the beaten down snow of the camp. Then, he lifted his nose to the air and smelled something burning. It smelled different than the smoke of a burning campfire. He trotted towards the smell and noticed that his friend's wagon was smoking. He knew that was not right. He ran up to the wagon and began barking furiously.

Suddenly, others awoke and looked out of their wagons to see what the commotion was all about. Coyote's wagon was the closest to Stan's, so when he looked out, he immediately saw what was wrong. He jumped out of his wagon quickly, to see what he could do.

Wheezer noticed that Stan was not coming out of the wagon, so he jumped up on the wheel, and then the front bench, to gain access to the front of the wagon. He lifted the cover sheet, with his nose, and upon entering, he saw that Stan was still lying fast asleep. Wheezer hopped down and began licking Stan's face and barking at intervals, finally, Stan began to stir and cough.

Just then, Coyote ripped the back sheet aside, to reveal the smoldering wooden bed of the wagon and knew just what to do. Coyote lowered the gate and grabbed a piece of wood that was lying nearby. He quickly scraped the burning coals out of the wagon and into the snow, then, he scooped up armfuls of snow, to pack onto the burning wood of the wagon floor.

"Stan, are you alright in there?" asked Coyote.

"Yes, I think so. Wheezer got me up, just in time. Thank you for your help. I don't know how a fire would get started at the back of my wagon. I don't smoke in the wagon," said Stan, while coughing.

"I know. This was not caused by you, it was a deliberate attempt to burn your wagon and maybe you as well, Stan," said Coyote.

Wheezer was busy licking Stan's face, getting all the soot off of it. Coyote noticed Wheezer, and was pleased he had raised the alarm.

"If Wheezer had not barked when he did, your wagon would be ablaze by now," said Coyote.

Stan got up from his bed, to survey the damage. All in all, it was not bad. There was a terrible burn mark on the floor of the wagon, but nothing else was damaged. He thanked God that he had not lost his life that night. He stepped down from the wagon, while others had come, to look to see what had happened. Coyote drew Stan to the side, to talk to him.

"Stan, I think Phineas did this. I think he has caught up with the train. We need to be on our guard even more. This proves, he will stop at nothing to hurt you and maybe even the train," said Coyote.

"But, how could a man alone have made it all this way? I mean, we crossed two deserts and those other mountains. How could he have kept up with us?" asked Stan.

"Determination, Stan. He is determined to get revenge, even though the wagon was yours to begin with. He is not right in the head. My people would have cast him out, but they would not have hurt him either. It takes a man with much willpower, to go through what he has endured. I imagine he hates you with a passion, by now. I think, we should put your wagon in the middle of the train, from now on. Maybe, that will make it harder for him to cause you further damage," said Coyote.

Wheezer barked his approval and wagged his tail. Coyote knew that Wheezer would take it upon himself, to guard the camp, even more during the night.

"Wheezer, you did very good. You saved Stan's life tonight. We could not ask for a better friend than you," said Coyote.

They would continue on the next day and the next, braving the cold and ice, to get to the other side of the Sierra Nevada mountains, before the heavy snows fell.

Chapter 26

On day five of being in the mountains, a party of soldiers approached from the west. They were on a rescue mission, to help the trains that were coming up behind the Cherokees. Many of them were mired in the snow and unable to move on the east side of the mountain. The soldiers carried needed supplies and food to the travelers, which were in dire, desperate, straits.

The commander had given them more advice, on the best way down the mountain, and it seemed that they were very close to their goal. The soldiers continued on to the east and the train traveled with renewed vigor.

However, the group of soldiers happened upon one man alone, traveling with barely any food to speak of and the commander stopped him.

"Sir, what are you doing out here alone? You could die out here," said the commander.

"I got separated from my group, while I was out hunting. I'm hurrying to catch up with them. I think you may have seen them. They are the ones, with all the Cherokees. I wonder if you could help me out some, before you get going. I need some food and a blanket. Anything you could do, would help me catch up to them," said Phineas.

"Certainly sir, I will be happy to. That is what we are out here for. We just did not expect to find, one man alone. You will find your group, not far ahead, but on foot it might take you a couple of days to catch up. Here are some supplies and the blanket you asked for. I think there is coffee, a little sugar, some flour, baking powder and some bacon. That ought to last you a few days travel," said the commander.

With that the soldiers continued on, to help others in need, and Phineas smiled to himself. God must be with him and approved of his mission. He did not know the results of the fire he set in Stan's wagon. He was sure he had created devastation, though, and it made him happy to think of it. He would not try to catch up to the wagon train, until they reached the goldfields, and if the opportunity presented itself, he would do all he could to wipe them out.

*****

The train was on the downhill side of the mountain. The trail caused the wagons to sway back and forth. There were rocks as big as boulders on the trail and some of them had to be cleared away, so the train could continue on. One of the wagons had tried to steer clear, of a protruding rock, when one of the wheels smashed up against it and broke the wheel. They were forced to stop, to make repairs. It was not a catastrophe, because one of the other wagons had an extra wheel. They just had to take the time to replace it and then they would be on their way.

If the weather held, they would be able to make Lassen's Rancho, by the next day, and from there, they could all decide, where in the goldfields they would like to try. Once they reached the rancho, it would be, every man for him-self, and the company would dissolve.

Rev. Piney was also on the downhill side, in fact, not far from the train, but he held back. He did not want to be seen in daylight. He was getting so close to the goldfields, that he could almost taste it. Finally, after all he had gone through, he would reach his goal and the gold would be his.

It never occurred to him that he would have a hard time digging it out with only one working arm, but his dreams, only allowed for success.

As the train continued on to their destination, the snows began anew, only heavier. It seemed that they were getting there, in the nick of time. The next day saw them struggling through the snow and down into the open, on the west side of the mountains. A little further along and they came to Lassen's Rancho. From here, they would hear of where the diggings were and what supplies they would need to buy. Peter Lassen had promoted his route, for that very purpose.

The train camped just down the road from the rancho and the group got together to discuss, what they all wanted to do next.

"I would like to stick with Coyote and Sasa, if they don't mind. I imagine that one place will be as good as another and there is safety in numbers. What do you say Coyote?" said Stan.

"Sasa and I have no objection at all. In fact, we would like it very much. What about the rest of you?" said Coyote.

Some of the group planned to go their own way and some banded together with another wagon. The rancho is where they would split, and go in different directions, to make their claims. Some would travel further south, closer to Sutter's fort. That was the direction that Coyote and Stan had determined to go.

The next day, they came up to Lassen's Rancho to get advice and buy supplies.

"Well, howdy folks! Mighty glad, to see ya. Glad you made it over them mountains. Did you have any trouble up there?" asked Lassen.

"Just the normal wear and tear on our wagons. We need to buy supplies and we also need some advice. Can you tell us what we will need to harvest the gold?" asked Coyote.

Sasa was looking at some of the goods. She was appalled at the prices, especially the cost of flour which was about ten times, what it was back home.

"These prices are outrageous," said Sasa.

"No, not for here, they ain't. It's supply and demand here. It's hard to get this stuff here, so you have to pay the price. It ain't no cheaper down at Sutter's, neither," said Lassen.

"So, what are we going to need?" asked Sasa.

"Outside of the food stuffs you want, you will need a pan for the gold. Or, some of the men is startin' to use a rocker, to separate the gold from the dirt. This here is one of them. This one is twenty-four dollars. Built real well and works like a charm," said Lassen.

The cost took Sasa's breath away, but Coyote did not seem to be surprised.

"Then you're gonna need a pick-ax, a shovel and maybe a hand pick as well," said Lassen.

Thankfully, Coyote and Sasa had brought some of those things with them, but Stan had not. Stan ended up buying the pick-ax. Both Coyote and Stan bought pans, for panning the gold. Neither of them, had any experience with a rocker, so they decided to not buy one, until they saw how it worked.

After buying what food stuffs they could afford, they headed down the trail toward the Sacramento River. They would follow that trail down to Sutter's Fort and then go to find their claims. In the excitement, of finally making it to California and over the Sierra Nevada, they failed to remember the lone traveler that followed them.

*****

Upon reaching Lassen's Rancho, Rev. Piney was exhausted, to the point of collapse, but he would not hear of stopping to rest. Mr. Lassen offered, to take a look at his black and limp arm, which had not pained him much in the cold, but he had no patience for sitting down and letting Lassen examine him.

"Now mister, I think you won't get much further with that arm that away. Somethin' like that could poison your whole body, and then some," said Lassen.

"I don't care and I won't let this dead arm slow me down! I aim to keep up with some immigrants that passed through here this morning. I have a few things I need and then I will be gone, so let's get on with it," said Rev. Piney.

Phineas had no idea that the arm was beginning to sicken him. At his shoulder, there were red streaks that emanated, from the blackened part of his upper arm. The streaks stretched across his chest and down to his abdomen, but he never looked at them. He was a man consumed with hate. Even Lassen's warning, fell on deaf ears.

With his few remaining dollars, he purchased another mule, but this time, he would ride it instead of walking beside it. He also bought some basic food stuffs, but no mining equipment, not even a pan for panning gold. He had believed the stories that the gold would be on the ground, where you could just, reach down and pick it up. He didn't see a need, for any of the tools Lassen was selling.

He had only been at Lassen's, for about three hours and was now, far down the trail. Lassen had told him that some of the wagons had split off from the train, to go their own ways, but with careful questions, Phineas found out that Coyote and Stan were headed for Sutter's Fort. That was the trail he was on now.

As the day darkened, the snow continued to fall, so he pulled over to the side of the trail to make camp. He found a small clearing that was sheltered by hills and rocks and began to build a fire. There were trees and saplings all around, so he set about pulling down the lower dead limbs and breaking them off for firewood. But, the snow on the limbs, threatened to smother his fire and he had to continually keep stoking it. Even so, it did not sustain bright flames, but smoked and smoldered. It looked, as if, he would have to sleep in a cold camp this night.

He got up to go outside of camp, to relieve him-self, giving no thought at all about his surroundings. Because his fire continued to smoke, he was in no danger of getting lost, but he had not taken anything along for protection. On his way back to his camp, he suddenly heard a scream, like that of a woman. It was quite close and the sound coursed through his body. His skin rippled with gooseflesh and the hair at the nap of his neck, stood on end.

Was there a woman out here? She sounded so close, why can't he spot her camp and other people? When the sound came again, he heard a snarl at the end. This could not be a real woman. Then what? He dare not call out. He realized he had left camp, without so much as a knife. Quickly he made his way back, to his smoldering fire, but the fire had gone out.

At that moment something heavy hit him and knocked him down, something, warm and furry. He grabbed for his knife, by the dead campfire and swung around to meet his attacker, but he could not see anything, in the gloom of the evening and the falling snow. Then the sound came again, this time very close and he realized, he was being hunted, by a mountain lion. He had seen them before, back in the forests of Arkansas, but they never tried to attack. This one was much bigger than the ones at home, and Phineas was sure it was trying to make its kill, for the night.

The cat circled around, to come at him, from a different direction. Without warning, it pounced on him, biting into the blackened shoulder of his bad arm. He screamed out, with pain and anger. Savagely, Phineas swung his knife, in an upward thrust, into the stomach of the great cat and it fell off of him. Snarling at him, it made its way back into the wilderness, to lick its wounds or die.

Phineas, too was left with wounds, but where the cat had bitten him was strangely devoid of blood. He stoked the fire and the coals began to gleam. He looked at his shoulder. Only the holes were left and some type of fluid flowing out of them. In the gloom, he could not make out what it was, but he could see that the liquid was not dark like blood. The stench sickened his stomach, as he ban-daged his wounds with a cotton cloth.

He had tied his mule to a nearby tree, so he went over to see if the cat had also attacked it, but the mule was fine, it was only frightened and skittish. He calmed the mule with his good hand and then stumbled back to his blanket. He fell into a deep exhausted sleep and woke the next day, covered in six new inches of snow. He was stiff and sore from his encounter with the cat, but he would not allow it to keep him from catching up to, Stan Grant and Coyote.

Chapter 27

Stan, Coyote and Sasa traveled on for several days. Because of the snow, the traveling went slower. They had to be careful, not get stuck in a drift, because the rest of the train had either gone on or split off, to look for gold and that left only the three of them, to push the wagons out. They followed along the Sacramento River, when they could, but would leave it, when bluffs and rocky hills got in the way. They didn't try to travel in a hurry, they knew, that mistakes would be made, if they did not take it slow. That night, they camped by a high bluff, overlooking the river.

Wheezer and Yellow Eyes played in the snow, but when it got too cold for Wheezer, he hopped up into the wagon and snuggled under the blankets. The cold did not bother Yellow Eyes, so without Wheezer to play with, he went hunting. He backtracked the way they had come the day before and his nose told him that something was dead, close by. He sniffed out the odor and followed the scent, to a group of pines. Behind the pines was a small burrow. He checked all around the entrance and finally decided to go inside.

Yellow Eyes slithered into the hole, deep inside, he found a dead mountain lion. He grabbed it by the scruff of the neck and pulled it out, into the open. He was fed regularly by Coyote, so he was not hungry, but he did not want to give up his prize. He looked up at the trail and looked back at the cat, deciding to drag it to the camp and present it to Coyote. Little by little he dragged the carcass toward camp. It took him over two hours, to get there with the cat.

Coyote was tending the cook fire, and Stan and Sasa were talking, next to the wagons. It would be time to bed down for the night, soon. Yellow Eyes grabbed hold of the cat again and dragged it over to Coyote.

"What in the world is this?" asked Coyote.

Yellow Eyes looked up at Coyote with loving eyes. Coyote examined the cat and found a wound on it abdomen, under its ribcage.

"Boy, you didn't do this. Where did you find it?" said Coyote.

Sasa walked over to see, what Coyote and Yellow Eyes were looking at.

"What is it Coyote? Oh, a Mountain Lion! Did Yellow Eyes kill it? Boy is it big," said Sasa.

"No, I think he found it. This is a knife wound, in its gut. I guess ole Yellow Eyes presented it to me. I could skin it, since it is still pretty fresh. It would make a nice coat. It is big enough to make one for you, Sasa. I'll get started on it right away. In the meantime, I would be thankful if you would rig up a drying frame for the pelt, when I am done" said Coyote.

But Coyote, wondered how the cat had been stabbed in the gut. Who was responsible for it and where were they now? He deftly skinned the cat, rubbed the cats brains into the flesh side of the skin, and once it was stretched on a drying frame, he propped it up in the wagon. There it would stay for several days, while he continued to scrap the fat off of the inside of the skin. Then, he would work the hide with his hands, pulling and stretching until it was supple. It was a very old method, for curing the skin of any warm-blooded animal, and it would make a long lasting pelt, for the coat he would make for Sasa.

After a few more days of travel, they finally made it to Sutter's Fort, early in the morning. They were elated to hear, that other Cherokee had already been through, and had made it safely to the diggings. Coyote, Sasa and Wheezer entered the store, followed closely by Stan.

"Hello friends," said Mr. Sutter. "Your welcome to browse the store and any advice I have, I give freely. You can file for your claims, here if you like, and I will see to it, that the claim gets filed in the proper place. It will save you a trip to Sacramento or San Francisco. Sacramento is closer, but is basically new. My boy, John Augustus Sutter, Jr. founded it on an embarcadero that I constructed, several years ago, at the Sacramento and American juncture of the rivers. There is a small assayer's office there, and a place to file your claim. But, if your claim is closer to San Francisco, there is a much bigger office there."

"Thank you kindly. Where is a good place to look for a claim? We don't know where to start. We want to stake our claims side by side, with our friend here, Stan Grant. We are Coyote and Sasa, by the way. Glad to meet you," said Coyote.

"Well now, I've heard good things about goin' up the Middle Fork of the American River. Not many have been up there, so far. I'm afraid that the South Fork of the American River, are getting' kinda crowded these days. That would be my best advice to ya. If'n you're a needin' any tools, you can get'em here, if'n you like. If you all want to wait to file your claim, until you actually find whatcha all are lookin for, then just stack a pile of rocks with a note inside, that describes your claim and that will work for the time bein. Then, hurry on up here, file it official like and then skedaddle on back, afore someone takes it," said Mr. Sutter.

*****

The next morning, Rev. Piney guided his mule up the incline, to Sutter's Fort. The man there was helpful, but seemed suspicious.

"Say young man, you really need to get that arm looked at by a bona-fide doctor. That don't look good at'tal. The closest doc is in Sacramento, just down the river some. But, it looks as if you been nursin' that arm, for some time," said Mr. Sutter.

Phineas looked down at his arm and at the stain from his leaking wounds, on his shoulder and shook his head.

"It will be fine. I've got other, more important things to do, before I get to a doctor. Maybe after I stake my claim, I can go searching for a doc. I will be back when I find my claim. Say, did two Indians and a white man come this way?" said Rev. Piney.

Mr. Sutter brightened at the memory of the nice people he had met. He liked to see Indians, getting their fair share of the gold.

"They sure nuff did, mister. Early this morning,' bout eight. If'n you hurry, you might be able to catch'em, long bout sundown. I think they were going ta the Middle Fork of the American," said Mr. Sutter.

Phineas stared at Mr. Sutter, to see if he saw any deception in him, but he only saw sincerity.

"You wouldn't be lying to me now, would you?" asked Rev. Piney.

"What in blue blazes, do you think I am? Tarnation, I would not last long in business, if'n I led people astray, all the time. I think, maybe you better get on your way," said Mr. Sutter, perturbed.

After a brief time at the store, Phineas took his mule and headed for the Middle Fork, with directions from Mr. Sutter, begrudgingly given. He made it to the junction of the three forks of the American, and noticed a great amount of activity, along the South Fork. He took the middle of the three forks and worked his way along, but he was feeling dizzy now and sick, so he made camp.

The cat wounds at his shoulder, continued to ooze pus that ran down his chest. Even though it was cold and the snow was all around, he stepped to the shore, removed his sling and shirt, and splashed water on his shoulder, to rinse off the old pus. The stench was becoming unbearable. He then rinsed out his sling and shirt, barely feeling the cold on his skin.

He built his campfire, and laid his wet clothes beside it to dry. He wore only his coat, over his naked shoulders, while he made his evening meal, of bacon and biscuits. Then he leaned back on a boulder and quickly fell asleep.

He was suddenly awakened, by the voice of a stranger.

"Well now, what do we have here? Are you all by yourself, mister?" asked the stranger.

Phineas started to get up, but the man signaled him to sit back down, so he did. Phineas was frightened somewhat, but not sure if the man meant to do him harm or not.

"My name is White, Mr. Sam White from Kentucky. I got me a claim, just up the river here. I was acomin' back from getting supplies, when I seen your fire. Say, you've got a bad arm there. It sure looks bad, mister," said the Mr. White.

Phineas thought for a moment. Sometimes, the fact that he was a reverend kept him safe. Most people would not harm, a man of the cloth.

"I am Rev. Phineas Piney. I'm with some other people, they should be here soon," lied Phineas.

"Sure nuff? Well, that is mighty fine. I been hankerin' for some company. Been up here for about two months and folks is just now acomin' to the Middle Fork. Pickins is pretty good here, but not as good as the South Fork. But, if'n you want on the South Fork, you gotta traipse a mighty long way to find a claim, where no one ain't already aworkin'. Now, my claim is pretty good. I figger, I'll clean it out, then move on up to another spot, stake another claim. You staked your claim yet, Reverend?" said Mr. White.

"Not yet. I'm just now looking around for a place. Any advice?" said Phineas, still suspicious.

"Well, there are some mighty nice places to dig on up the river. Pick a place with lots of gravel and do some pannin', before you stake your claim to it. If'n nothin' comes from the pannin', then move on. But chances are, you'll find your share of gold. Now me, I been takin' about three, four ounces a day and that's pretty fair. Work steady and build it up. You'll have your fortune in no time at'all. I take my poke down to ole Mr. Sutter's Fort. He has a safe there, and he'll keep your stash, until you're ready to take it to San Francisco, to bank it. Say, how you a gonna dig and pan with only one good arm?" said Mr. White.

Phineas had not been thinking about that. He was so intent, on causing harm to Stan Grant and his friends, that he never thought about his injured arm.

"I'll muddle through, I expect. Thanks for the advice. It's time I turned in. Got a long day ahead of me, tomorrow," said Phineas.

Mr. White's smile left his face.

"That's not very neighborly of you Reverend. You could at least offer me a cup a coffee. Seems like, we is gonna be neighbors for a time. What do ya say?" said Mr. White.

Phineas saw no way out of it. So without argument, he grabbed his tin cup and poured the man some coffee and handed it over. The man sat, as the smile returned to his face.

"Now, that is more like it. Nothing like a hot cup a coffee, when it's cold out, and your bones need a warmin'. I'm supposin', that you think I'm here ta rob ya. Well, ain't nothin' further from the truth. Why should a man rob, when gold is right underneath his feet. No sir, I wouldn't rob ya. Just wanted a cup of that coffee and if'n you don't mind, I'll bed down here for the night and then be on my way back to my claim in the mornin'," said Mr. White.

The next day, Phineas breathed a sigh of relief, when the man was true to his word, and trudged off down the river bank.

*****

The two wagons found the going very slow and almost impossible. They had traversed the land, back from the shoreline, when the rocks made it too difficult to use the wagons, but now they decided to stop and test the gravel. They unhitched the oxen, to lead them to water and made camp. Sasa pulled out the pans they bought from Mr. Sutter and slipped down to the water with Coyote, to try to do some panning. It was not hard, only repetitive, but it was no time at all, when they began to find nice size nuggets in the pans.

"Look at this Coyote. I never dreamed it would be so easy," said Sasa.

"I imagine it will be easy, until we glean all the surface gold off. Then we will have to dig down, in the icy water, to get to the gold. I saw this type of mining, on my way down to Indian Territory. It will get harder and harder. I suppose the trick will be, to glean what we can off the top, and then move to another unworked claim. However, I think the larger nuggets will be buried in the gravel, so digging can be very profitable. If we do that, we will need one of those rockers that Mr. Lasson tried to sell to us. I believe, I saw a few of them at Sutter's Fort. We can pick one up, when one of us goes back to file our claims," said Coyote.

Stan joined them at the shore.

"Hey, that looks promisin'. Let's stake our claims, side by side, right here. There's room for our wagons and grass for our oxen. We can stay a little while, at least," said Stan.

Then Sasa climbed up the embankment and up onto a small bluff, to look over what they would be making a claim to. It did have all the necessary things to make a good camp. She turned and looked upriver and downriver. She could just make out a lonely traveler coming from the west, but he was so far away, she could not say how many people there were, or who it might be. She didn't think much of it. They were bound to come in contact with many other gold seekers, the longer they stayed here, so she put it out of her mind.

Stan made his claim on the east side of Sasa and Coyote's. Then, Sasa realized that she could make a claim as well. So she claimed the area to the west of Coyote's. Now, they possessed three claims that they would each work. Stan's claim had a high bluff, close to the shoreline, which gave him some shelter from the elements. They could all pan, but winter was still bearing down on them, and eventually they would have to make some shelter.

Coyote began, by allowing Sasa to pan, while he felled some trees, to make a cabin for the three of them. When

Sasa took a break from her chores, she walked up to the trees where Coyote was working and sat down on a stump.

"Coyote, we need to talk," said Sasa.

Sasa's eyes gleamed with excitement.

"Sure, aren't we talking right now?" asked Coyote.

"No, I mean I want to talk to you about something important. You need to stop working and come over and sit here," said Sasa.

"Alright, I'm here. Is there something wrong? Did something happen?" asked Coyote.

"Yes, something happened and no, nothing is wrong. Something is very right, but maybe not at a good time," said Sasa.

"You aren't making any sense, Sasa. What are you trying to say?" said Coyote.

"I've been keeping this a secret until we reached our claim. Now we are here, I think you should know, that we are expecting a little Coyote," said Sasa.

But, Coyote still did not understand.

"Little Coyote? What on earth are you talking about, Sasa. What do you mean, little Coyote? We don't need another, we have Yellow Eyes and he is enough," said Coyote.

Sasa heaved a sigh of frustration.

"No, I mean, we are going to have a baby, Coyote. Our own little Coyote," said Sasa, smiling.

Coyote was struck dumb, for a moment, and then began whooping and shouting at the top of his voice. Stan heard and came running, thinking something was wrong. When they told him, he joined Coyote in the celebration. Then it dawned on Coyote where they were. He then knew that their cabin would have to be a bit bigger, so that Sasa could have some privacy. It was either that or he go hunting and kill some buffalo to make enough skins for a tipi. But the trees were there and were more practical, because they were in the mountains, where buffalo did not roam. He started back at his work of chopping down trees, with more vigor and Stan took his own axe and began to help Coyote.

Sasa told Coyote that she had found she was pregnant, just before they entered the salt desert, by the Mormons Salt Lake, about the last of September. It was now the first week of November. That meant, she was at least four months along. She would give birth in the Spring. She was totally happy, but not as worried as Coyote was, already.

The group panned and worked on the cabin at intervals, while Wheezer and Yellow Eyes patrolled the shore and surrounding hills, for vermin.

Chapter 28

Rev. Piney had followed, as close as he dared. When the group stopped to make their claim, he also stopped, made camp and waited. Soon, one of them would have to leave, to stake their claim at Sutter's, and he would be ready. He felt sick now, most of the time, and even though he had little pain, he was weak and feverish. He gave little thought to staking his own claim. His whole mind was set on revenge. The weather was getting colder, and soon he would need some type of shelter. But, how could he build a shelter with only one arm? He did not dwell on the problem.

Periodically, he crept close to Coyote's campsite to watch. Finally, he noticed that Coyote was packing his saddlebags. He must be getting ready to go file his claim. Phineas was going to have to act quickly, if he was going to follow. He went back to his camp and packed a small bag and his gun. He would not take his mule. He did not want to be spotted. When Coyote left camp, headed for Sutter's Fort, Phineas waited a bit and then followed. He planned on catching Coyote unexpectedly, with no one to witness it.

About midday, Coyote took a break to eat, rest, and play a while with Yellow Eyes, who had accompanied him. To gain an advantage point, Phineas climbed up and settled into some boulders, about fifty feet away. He was sweating profusely and his eyes blurred, but he watched Coyote carefully. He readied his pistol, to take his shot and waited. Coyote was finished eating and was repacking his saddlebags, when the shot rang out. Coyote went down hard and Phineas smiled. He climbed down from the rocks, disappeared into the brush and headed back to his camp. He did not notice the form that followed him, from place to place.

Now, there would only be two people left in camp and if he was careful, he could get them as well. But first, he needed to rest. The exertion was getting to him and he lacked the energy to hurry. He found his camp, which was concealed in the rocks, away from prying eyes. He waited until the sun started to go down, before he moved towards the other camp.

*****

Stan had been cutting more trees for the cabin and had come back to camp, for the evening meal. They did not expect Coyote to be back that night and maybe not the next day either. In the meantime, Sasa would pan, what was turning out to be a very profitable claim. They kept the campfire burning continuously, to help battle the cold. Wheezer lay close to its warmth. The sky was overcast, but the snow held off from falling, for several days. That gave them time to work on the cabin.

But Sasa was worried. She had no real reason to be, but she remembered seeing the person or persons, who seemed to be following them. She had not seen anyone since, and it could just be, a coincidence and the person or persons, might just be gold seekers. However, Sasa felt apprehensive all the same. She wished she had gone with Coyote to make the claims and she worried for his safety. She made an effort, to put it out of her mind, while she continued clearing up the evening meal.

Stan was stashing his tools in the wagon and stowing his poke of gold. Sasa was at the shore rinsing off the plates and dirty pan, she cooked in. when she saw something out of the corner of her eye. It was a movement, furtive and slow. Sasa turned towards it and was brought up short by a gun, now pointed at her chest, only twenty feet away.

"What do you want?" asked Sasa.

Wheezer caught sight of the man and began to growl.

"Call Mr. Grant. Tell him, you have something to show him," said Phineas.

"No, I won't," said Sasa.

But, it was too late. Stan came down from the wagon, just then, and approached Sasa, not noticing the man hidden in the shadows.

"What's wrong with Wheezer?" asked Stan.

"Mr. Grant, welcome to our party. You won't mind, if'n I make myself at home. After tonight, I'll not only have that wagon back, I'll have your claims as well," said Phineas.

"How do you figure that? Coyote will track you down. You can't escape," said Stan.

"Ha, ha, no he won't. I already done him in. He's headed, for wherever Indians go, when they die," laughed Phineas.

Sasa gasped. The pain in her heart was sharp. She could barely breathe.

"I don't believe you," said Sasa.

"Don't matter none, if'n you don't. You won't be around, anyway, to worry about it. I might even be, do'n you a favor," said Phineas.

As he was speaking, another shadow loomed up out of the darkness, and came up behind Sasa and Stan. Wheezer began to bark furiously, and was swept aside. When Phineas saw the newcomer, he began to back up towards the shelter of Stan's camp, and its rocky overhang. It was obvious, he was frightened, but he still, was able to maintain a smile, upon his face.

When Sasa and Stan turned, as one, to look behind them, they immediately fell to the side, and lay still, while Phineas continued to back up. Only the rocks stopped him, from his backward retreat, and the smile left his face.

"No! No! You can't be real. Leave me alone! I ain't done nothin' to you. Go on, get! You, get on outta here, now!" yelled Phineas.

But, the figure, lunged at Phineas, and a mighty growl, came out of a large, slobbering mouth, full of sharp teeth. Phineas fired his gun, but to no avail. The grizzly bear, came down, with all its body weight, on top of Phineas. He screamed in pain, then, the bear stood up again. It reached out, with its mighty claws, and raked the rock face, of the overhang. Rocks began to fall; just a few, at first. Then, a great rumble sounded, as the entire rock face dropped down on top of Rev. Phineas Piney, burying him under several feet of rock and large boulders.

Suddenly, Wheezer came out of the gloom, and bounded at the bear, biting him on his abdomen, and forelimbs. Wheezer landed a good bite, into the bear's flesh, and held on for life itself. The bear whirled around, so violently, that it slung Wheezer off, and he took a mouthful of bear fur with him. Then, just as unexpectedly, the bear slowly turned, and went shambling off, into the darkness, to lick its wounds.

Sasa and Stan sat up, looked at each other, and wondering what had just happened, before their very eyes. Wheezer was also up, checking on Sasa.

"Have you ever seen a bear, so big? I've heard of grizzly bears before, but I never thought they were, so huge," said Stan.

"I am used to black bears. But, I've never seen a grizzly before, and I don't want to see another one," said Sasa.

Sasa, suddenly realized what Phineas had told her, and jumped up quickly, to pack a traveling bag.

"I've got to go, and find Coyote. Phineas said, he killed him, but I don't believe it," said Sasa.

"It's best if you go first thing in the morning, Sasa. You can't see what is out there in the dark. You will be able to see his tracks in the daylight," urged Stan.

Sasa thought it through, for a moment, then, came to the same conclusion. She would wait until dawn before going to look for her beloved Coyote.

After a sleepless night, Sasa made the morning coffee and readied herself to go. Then, she noticed a figure, and what looked like a dog, coming along the river, from the west. When the figures got closer, Sasa realized, they were Coyote and Yellow Eyes. His head was bandaged and he progressed slowly, but he came at a steady pace. Sasa ran, and put her arms around him, depositing tears on his neck. After a time, he pulled her away.

"No need to cry, I'm here. I believe Phineas tried to kill me. The bullet grazed my head, but I fell and laid still. I was lucky that he did not come to check. Tell me, is everyone alright here? Have you seen him? " asked Coyote.

"Yes and no. Phineas is dead. Come and see and I will explain what happened," said Sasa.

After telling him, all that had transpired, Coyote went over to the pile of rocks that had once been an overhang, on Stan's claim. Coyote bent down in deep contemplation, then, he picked up a rock to examine it. Excitedly, he jumped up and ran to Stan.

"Stan, look! Look at this! That overhand was full of gold! The rocks have a clear vein of gold, running through them," said Coyote.

Stan was absolutely stunned. Then, a quiet smile, spread across his face.

"I guess Phineas, finally got what he wanted, his share of the gold. I'll be happy to divide the gold, in the rocks, with you, if'n you will help me uncover Phineas and give him a proper burial, over by the slope of the mountain. I'm sure sorry he got to you. I don't suppose, you were able to file our claims, did you?" said Stan.

"No, I came right back here, after I got shot. I was worried about you and Sasa. Sure, I will be happy to help, but I think that you should hurry and file all our claims, before anyone sees, what we have found. That will give me a chance to recoup," said Coyote.

Wheezer came over to Coyote, nuzzled Yellow Eyes, and then licked Coyote on the hand, welcoming him, back to camp.

Chapter 29

The small cabin, served them well. They finished it, just in time for the hard snows. While winter dragged on, Stan and Coyote busied themselves, building two rockers that would separate the gold from the dirt. Eventually, they would have to begin digging, when all the surface gold was taken out. Sasa was busy making baby clothes, from material bought at Sutter's and skins, from the animals Coyote killed for food, especially rabbit fur.

Coyote determined, that they would work their claim, for the summer, and then they would be ready, to head back home, by the next spring. By that time, the Middle Fork, of the American River, would be full of other gold seekers. In fact, they had already met some late comers, who headed further east, along the river, to find their claims. People were coming from everywhere. They came by ship, to San Francisco, from the Canadian provinces, from Mexico, South America, and as far away as, Australia and Europe.

They had no idea what to expect, from the people that would come, to seek their fortunes. Mr. Sutter, was complaining, that the miners were already overrunning his land, stealing his cattle and making claims, of his land and waterways. It would be a matter of time, before law would break down completely, and Coyote did not want to be here, when that happened. Men, crazed for gold, were capable of many bad deeds and the fact that Coyote and Sasa were Indians, could, make trouble for them. It was not worth the gold, if something were to happen to Sasa and the baby. Until then, they would work their claims, save their gold, and be ready to abandon their claims, if need be.

Wheezer and Yellow Eyes went out daily to hunt and play, but Wheezer, never stayed out long in the cold. Sasa made a fur coat for Wheezer, which helped against the bitter winter cold, but his feet remained exposed, to the elements. He much preferred, to snuggle next to the fire, after his romp outside. Yellow Eyes always came back with something he had killed, and presented it to Coyote, who then skinned, whatever it was, and gave Yellow Eyes the meat.

Sasa was content to prepare, for the coming birth, but she secretly longed for home. The gold was incidental to her and she would have started for home, in the spring, if it were not for the baby coming. She thought sometimes, of all the Cherokees who started out with them on this journey and she wondered, if they found their fortunes. She knew that some, would come back home to Indian Territory, but a few would probably make their homes in California, rather than make the arduous trip back to Indian Territory. She hoped, she would get to see them again.

As for the Cherokee Trail the group of travelers had blazed, she knew that others now, were also, following that route. It made her proud that it was being used, by any one, who wanted to get to the gold fields of California, safely. During their entire trip, no one had died of Cholera and only one, had died of a disease. In this case, it had been diabetes. Maybe, another group of Cherokees would take that route, the next year, in 1850, to follow their dreams, of finding gold, in California.

She did not know, what awaited her in the years to come, but she had Coyote, Wheezer and Yellow Eyes. She would meet the challenges head on, like she did everything else.

Author's Note

Those of you that follow Wheezer's exploits, will know that Coyote and Sasa are fictional characters, and therefore, were not on that important trip to the goldfields. Wheezer is a real dog, but also was not there. However, in producing this book, I did my best, to follow the published diaries, of the travelers on that trip. The collected diaries are contained in a book. It is called, *"The Cherokee Trail Diaries"* Vol. 1, by Patricia K. A. Fletcher and Dr. Jack Earl Fletcher. It was very interesting reading, and included maps, of the entire journey.

Although, there was much racial conflict, there was no murder on that trip. However, I tried to bring out as much of the diaries, as I could work, into the story. Much of that route is now on private land, but some is accessible, to those who would like to see, where the group traveled. There are still wagon ruts visible to the naked eye, even after all these years.

I am sure that there were events on that wagon train that we will never know, because the writers of the diaries did not elaborate, in their writings. It is noteworthy, that the Fletchers did such a nice job, in bringing what was written in the diaries, to life.

You may ask, if this is the end of the story. The truth is, that I had to cut the book in half, because there was so much information that I could not contain it, in one book. You may very well see, the completion of this trip in the next volume of, Mysteries from the Trail of Tears.

As always, I will do my very best, to bring real, forgotten history, to life, so that, these events, will not be lost to time.

Wado
Kitty Sutton

Excerpts from actual diaries were taken from: *Cherokee Trail Diaries,* By Patricia K. A. Fletcher and Dr. Jack Earl Fletcher

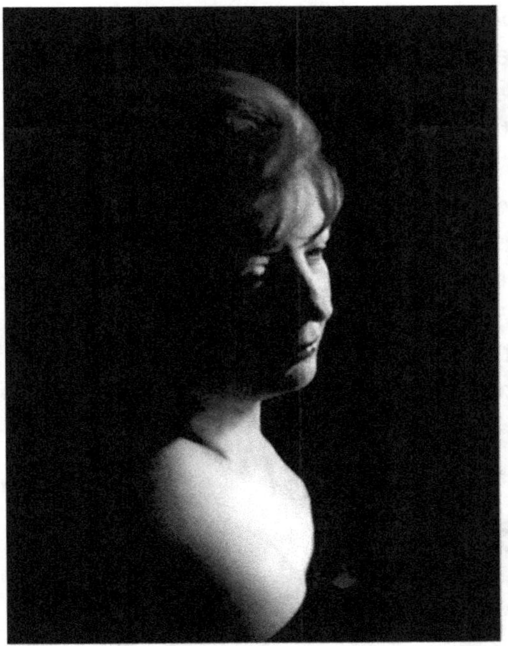

About the Author

Kitty Sutton was born Kathleen Kelley to an Osage/Irish family of professional musicians in Kansas City, Missouri, where Kitty was trained from an early age in dance, vocal, art and musical instruments. Her father was a Naval band leader. During the Great Depression, her mother helped to support her family by tap dancing in the speakeasys even though she was just a child; she was very tall for her age but made up like an adult. Kitty had music and art on all sides of her family which ultimately helped to feed her imaginative mind and desire to succeed.

Kitty married a wonderful Cherokee artist from Oklahoma, in fact the very area that she writes about in her Wheezer series of novels. After raising her family, Kitty came to Branson, Missouri and performed in her own one woman show there for twelve years. To honor her father, she performed under the name Kitty Kelley. She has three music albums and several original songs to her credit and is best known for her comical, feel good song called It Ain't Over Till The Fat Lady Sings. Kitty has been writing for many years and in 2011 Inknbeans Press accepted her manuscript of an historical Native American murder mystery. It was the first in a series of stories featuring Wheezer, a Jack Russell Terrier and his friend, Sasa, it is called, Wheezer And The Painted Frog. Kitty lives in the southwestern corner of Missouri near Branson with her husband of 40 years and her three Jack Russell Terriers, one of which is the real and wonderful Wheezer.

For the other books in the Mysteries of the Trail of Tears Series, and many other fine titles, visit www.kittysutton.weebly.com.

The Real Wheezer

If you enjoyed *Wheezer and the Road to Gold,* or if you have questions, or constructive criticism, you may contact Ms. Sutton at kittyandcompany@centurytel.net.

Wheezer and the Painted Frog, Wheezer and the Shy Coyote, Wheezer and the Golden Serpent, and *Wheezer and the Giveaway Child* can be found at fine booksellers everywhere.

Also, visit Kitty's website at:
www.kittysutton.weebly.com

Be sure to check out the other books by Kitty Sutton in this series.

Wheezer and the Painted Frog
Wheezer and the Shy Coyote
Wheezer and the Golden Serpent
Wheezer and the Giveaway Child

Little Buffalo Arts

Publishing

$15.99

ISBN 978-1-7321496-8-7

www.ingramcontent.com/pod-product-compliance
Lightning Source LLC
Chambersburg PA
CBHW071356100726
47908CB00004B/1006